As they rose higher, Kenzie said, "This is so beautiful. Thank you for sharing it with me."

"You're beautiful." Reed kissed her. Not the delicate first kiss he'd given her, but a more searching one, more passionate and filled with promise.

She caressed his cheek, her thoughts in turmoil. She leaned against him, her head on his shoulder, and let all her cares drip away. This one moment was filled with promise and she wanted to savor it.

They stood, arms around each other as the balloon started to descend. As they stepped out of the gondola, an unusual shyness crept over Kenzie. She didn't know what to say or how to act. Reed studied her cautiously as though expecting to be rejected.

"I'm not quite sure how to tell you this…"

He stepped back, but she grabbed his hand and pulled him to her.

"I apologize. It was wrong of me to take advantage of the moment…"

"Stop." She held up her hand. "Stop. This was the most wonderful moment in my life. I want more. I want more with you."

Dear Reader,

Kenzie Russell is the last of the Russell clan to fall…
in love. Reed Watson, the last man she ever expected to
love, storms into her life and into her heart. He woos
her with a romantic dinner on Lake Tahoe and a fun
weekend at a comic book convention in San Francisco.
True love has twists and turns, peaks and valleys. Join
Kenzie and Reed as they negotiate the path to love with
humor and determination to discover the journey is as
sweet as the destination.

Jackie and I are sorry to see the end of the Russell family
saga. Next up on our docket is the Torres family, Scott's
in-laws and Nina's rambunctious siblings, as they venture
off in search of their ultimate happy endings. The first
story is set against the annual pageantry of the Pasadena
Tournament of Roses Parade featuring Daniel Torres and
Greer Courtland. Don't miss it.

Jackie and Miriam

J.M. Jeffries

DRAWING *Hearts*

J.M. Jeffries

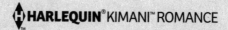

HARLEQUIN® KIMANI™ ROMANCE

Recycling programs
for this product may
not exist in your area.

ISBN-13: 978-0-373-86434-8

Drawing Hearts

Copyright © 2016 by Miriam A. Pace and Jacqueline S. Hamilton

This is a work of fiction. Names, characters, places and incidents are
either the product of the author's imagination or are used fictitiously,
and any resemblance to actual persons, living or dead, business establishments,
events or locales is entirely coincidental.

For questions and comments about the quality of this book please contact us
at CustomerService@Harlequin.com.

Printed in U.S.A.

Jackie and Miriam live in Southern California. When they aren't writing, Jackie is trying to take a nap and Miriam plays with her grandchildren. Jackie thought she wanted to be a lawyer until she met Miriam and decided to be a writer instead. Miriam always wanted to be a writer from her earliest childhood when she taught herself to read at age four. Both are avid readers and can usually be found with their noses in a book, or, now that it's the twenty-first century, their eReaders. Check out their blog at jmjeffries.com.

Books by J.M. Jeffries

Harlequin Kimani Romance

Virgin Seductress
My Only Christmas Wish
California Christmas Dreams
Love Takes All
Love's Wager
Bet on My Heart
Drawing Hearts

Visit the Author Profile page at
Harlequin.com for more titles.

To Rhonda: thank you so much for the wonderful years of friendship. You've been one of the best friends ever and thank you for letting me borrow your wonderful daughter. To Nikki: I watched you grow into an incredible woman. You are an inspiration.
All my love forever, Shar-Pei puppy love.
—Jackie

To Warrick Aurelian Pace: such a huge name for such a small baby. I know you will live up to it and be as amazing as your cousins, Kathryn and Frederik Stein.
To Erin Pace: thank you for my new grandbaby and letting me bounce ideas off you.
To Jeff Pace: thank you for being you.
To Miriam Pace Stein: you are such an amazing mother.
I'm so proud of all of you.
—Miriam

Acknowledgments

Thank you to Shannon Criss
and the entire Harlequin staff.
They provide us with wisdom, knowledge and care.

A special thank-you to the Harlequin Art Department
for the best covers ever.

All of you rock!

Chapter 1

Kenzie Russell wanted to pound her laptop with her fists. The software she'd commissioned for the boutiques refused to work and Nina, perched on a stool with one leg crossed over the other, grinned at her frustration. The big flashy diamond on Nina's left hand winked as the morning sun streamed through the open patio doors. Splashing and laughter drifted up from the pool far below.

"Explain to me how this software works," Nina said, taking a sip of her iced tea.

Kenzie wasn't certain how it worked, but she knew how she wanted it to work. "A customer enters the boutique and doesn't find anything. This software will allow a clerk to take a photo of the customer, input the photo and the body measurements and then allow them to try on clothes in a virtual environment. The clothes would expand or contract depending on the body type. I've lined up a dozen designers who are ready to try this and I can't make it work." She tried not to give in to the urge to unleash her frustration out on the counter. She scowled at the screen.

"Sounds complicated."

Her best friend wasn't helping. "I'm sure the software engineer I dealt with understood my instructions." She knew she'd been explicit enough; she'd even written down what she'd wanted so he wouldn't misunderstand.

"I'm sure he did," Nina replied.

Kenzie glared at her best friend. They'd been friends since college when they'd roomed together. "It has to work."

"Maybe you need a hammer."

"You're not helping." A hammer sounded good, but she didn't think the laptop would survive. Kenzie turned back to the screen. "Let's try again."

Nina obediently stood and Kenzie activated the laptop's photo function. She pushed a button and the photo embedded itself into the viewer with the background stripped out. She'd already added Nina's dimensions. She tapped keys and once again the laptop froze. Kenzie ground her teeth in frustration. She'd thought her idea was brilliant, but the execution wasn't turning out the way she'd envisioned it.

"I think it's a great idea, but you have a few bugs to work out." Nina hopped back on her stool and reached for a muffin.

"Bugs? I have pterodactyls to work out."

"Why don't you ask Reed?"

"Number one, we haven't met. And how's that

going to sound? 'Hi, I'm Kenzie, can you fix the bugs in my software?'" That sounded so crass. He'd just arrived in Reno after months of dealing with family issues and here she was demanding help.

Nina chuckled. "He's very nice. I'm sure he'd be willing to help someone as lovely as you."

Kenzie growled. "You're responsible for this. You didn't want to try on wedding dresses."

"I'd love to try on wedding dresses, but I have no time." Nina sipped her coffee, unconcerned.

"I thought virtual wedding dresses were the answer." Kenzie had arranged with Vera Wang, Oscar de la Renta, Claire Pettibone and Carolina Herrera to take photos of wedding dresses so Nina could try them on in the virtual environment Kenzie developed for her. And once the idea took hold, Kenzie thought, it would work for other women. But the reality was turning out far different than she thought.

"It's a terrific idea," Nina said, "and I could spin this into a huge campaign, making the Casa de Mariposa a wedding destination."

"And you're envisioning…"

"We could have them try on their virtual wedding gowns in their home and have the gown waiting for them when they arrive as part of the whole package. And we could do this with the groom and the bridesmaids and the groomsmen. And if the bride doesn't want to buy a gown, we'll rent it to her. There are so many variations on the idea that I can't stop thinking about it." Nina picked up her iPad and started typing.

"Give you a bit of rope and you become a cowgirl."

"I'd rather have glass slippers and be Cinderella. You know how I feel about nature." Nina licked muffin crumbs off her fingers and took a long sip of her iced tea.

"Your idea of camping is a suite at the Waldorf Astoria."

Nina simply grinned, pointing at her face. "This is my, 'Oh, I'm so ashamed' look. Your brother had the audacity to suggest we honeymoon on the Alaskan tundra."

"Doing what?" Kenzie asked curiously.

"Nature crap," Nina replied with a rich laugh.

"I assume you set him straight."

"I told him there would be no boom boom without a room. I would never be in the 'mood' in the outdoors."

Kenzie burst out laughing. The last person in the world she would have expected her brother, Scott, to hook up with was Nina. Yet she was thrilled. Nina got to be her legit sister, and life didn't get better than that.

Nina paused to admire the rock on her finger. Scott had terrific taste. The diamond was marquise-cut with emeralds along the sides.

Kenzie went back to her computer. She had Nina's photo on the screen and the pictures of wedding gowns on the side bar. She chose a gown to drag over to Nina's photo and then it happened. The screen pixelated and started to go wonky. Lines appeared, scrolling from side to side and Kenzie half screamed. "No. No. No. Stop. Stop. Stop."

The screen went blank.

"You hurt it," Nina said.

"I didn't do anything. Really." Kenzie frantically pushed keys, but the screen stayed stubbornly blank. She rubbed her forehead. This wasn't happening. Not now, when she so needed it to work.

"Can we hit it with a hammer now?" Nina asked, curiously. She bit into her muffin and smiled.

Kenzie didn't reply. If she'd had a hammer she would.

"Call Reed," Nina suggested. "Tell him to send someone here right away to save us. You can pull the granddaughter card." She slid off the stool and headed to the door with a wave. "Got to go. Catch you later."

"All right," Kenzie said, reaching for the in-house phone.

Reed Watson knocked on the door to the suite. From the other side of the door he could hear the menacing sound of someone muttering and snarling. That didn't sound good.

The door opened and Kenzie Russell stood there in all her beauty, wearing a red wrap dress that hugged her slender body like a glove. She was tall with curves in all the right places. Her brown hair was short and sort of spikey. His heart started racing and a bolt of heat hit him in the gut. And when she smiled at him her whole face lit up and he couldn't stop staring at her. She was that beautiful.

"Hi," she said, holding out her hand. "I'm Kenzie, and you are…?"

"Reed Watson."

"Oh, I'm so excited to meet you." She grabbed his hand and pulled him into her suite.

He looked down at her elegant hand in his, liking the way her silky cinnamon-colored skin looked against his whiteness. *Please don't let my palm start sweating.* He was reluctant to let her go. He took a deep breath to steady himself and inhaled the subtle scent of vanilla, spiced fig and orchid. She smelled delicious and exotic. He just wanted to bury his nose in her neck. A heated flush crept up his face and he forced himself to turn away and pretend to examine the decor.

The suite itself mirrored his with a living room, dining room and entry on one side and two bedrooms and a galley kitchen on the other, all opening to a balcony and a view of the mountains beyond. "I'm pleased to meet you, as well."

"You've been so elusive I thought you were an urban legend." She led him toward the dining table with paper scattered across the surface and her open laptop.

"My father has been ill and I needed to be with him." Chemotherapy did that to a person, but the last test results had shown the cancer in remission and Reed was finally able to get to Reno.

"Miss E. said you had family issues. I'm glad you're here now—I need your expertise." She gestured at her laptop. "It just stopped working."

He sat down at the table and tried to concentrate on the laptop with its blank screen. Anything to distract himself from her. "What's the problem?"

"It's broken."

"Broken in what way?"

She shrugged. "I don't know. You're the expert."

Okay, he thought. She was not a computer person. He glanced around and saw the disconnected power cord. He plugged it back into the computer, waited a few seconds and pressed the power button, and the laptop sprang back to life. It had just run out of battery power.

"How did you do that?" She stared at the flickering screen, one hand on her hip, the other pointing at the laptop.

"I have techno mojo." Most computer problems were simple. "It helps to have the power supply hooked up. Your battery ran out of power."

"That's all," she said.

He grinned. "That's all."

"So, you're a computer wizard." She leaned over his shoulder and slid her slender fingers over the mouse pad.

"I'm a god chained to Earth," he ended with a chuckle. He pushed the power cord tightly into the laptop.

She laughed. "Well, then, can you use your god-like qualities to make my software work?"

He liked that she liked his humor. "You're not a technophobe, are you?" he asked.

She frowned at him. "I know how to use my phone. I do everything on my phone." She held up the newest, top-of-the line iPhone.

"Explain the problem."

Leaning over his shoulder, she took the mouse and clicked on an icon. "I commissioned this program that will allow our boutique customers to try on clothes in a virtual environment, but the clothes won't adjust to figures properly and my computer freezes every time I try to drag something over."

For a moment he couldn't force his thoughts away from the way her soft skin brushed against his hand. He gulped. No one had told him how beautiful and sexy Kenzie Russell was. The throaty quality of her voice started his heart hammering away. He fought to breathe. Never in his whole adult life had he reacted to a woman like this.

Beautiful women had been throwing themselves at him since he'd made his first ten million. They'd been more attracted to his money than they were to him. At first, he'd been flattered, but later he'd grown jaded. Kenzie didn't seem to be looking at him in quite the same way. In fact, at the moment she wasn't looking at him at all as she frowned at her laptop.

"What do you want your software to do?" he asked when he found his voice again.

"I wanted the software to take a photo of the customer. A salesperson would input measurements and search for appropriate styles depending on what the customer wants." She waved a hand at the screen. "It seems so simple. Why can't it be simple?" She frowned at the laptop again.

If software was simple, he might be living in his dad's basement playing video games. "Who developed the software?"

"A friend of mine knew someone." She pulled a chair over and sat down next to him.

"The concept sounds interesting." He studied the laptop screen as she slid her fingers over the mouse pad and tried to show him. The laptop froze and she slapped her hand on the counter. He gently pushed her hand away and unfroze the screen.

"I know," she said eagerly. "Can you make it work? Miss E. says you can write software in your sleep. She says you can do anything."

"I don't know about 'anything.'" He laughed. "I like to work in my pajamas."

"You do?" She cast a sidelong glance at him. "I like

a man who can joke about wearing his pj's to work. For me, half the fun of going to work is dressing up."

"I know you're all about fashion." He opened the program again and began clicking through, trying to get a feel for it. From the way the program sputtered and lagged, he knew the code hadn't been very well written.

"How did you get into computers?" she asked, her dark brown eyes studying him.

"My father took me to a computer show in LA when I was around ten and bought all the components he'd need to build his own, because he figured it would be easy. Except it wasn't. After a couple hours of grunting and cursing, he started making dinner, and I put the computer together." Everything had fit exactly the way Reed had envisioned it. His father had been fascinated by Reed's intuitive understanding of the process.

"Pretty remarkable."

"Thank you." She sounded impressed. He liked that. Once he had that computer operating, he discovered what it could do and he'd decided to write his own game, which he'd distributed to his friends. And from there, he'd started his own company. In the years since, he'd worked in gaming, then moved to apps for smartphones, then into computer security, and his latest endeavor had been using computers to design prosthetic limbs. He'd immersed himself in his business until his father became ill. That was when he realized he was missing out on life.

"Have you fixed it yet?" Kenzie asked.

He chuckled. "This is going to take more than a few minutes."

"How much time?" She glanced at her watch. "I'm meeting my niece, she's teaching me to barrel-race."

He sat back in surprise, looking her up and down at her very fashionable dress, stiletto shoes and chunky necklace. He was having a hard time seeing her on a horse, wearing jeans, plaid shirt and cowboy boots.

"I know." She patted him on the hand.

"What do you mean?" he asked, confused.

"I can tell from the look on your face you are trying to picture me on a horse wearing boots and a Stetson."

"No...no... I wasn't thinking that exactly."

She laughed. "Sure you were. Just remember, I'm the girl with three older brothers. I may look like I stepped out of the pages of *Vogue* magazine every day, but at heart I'm pretty much a tomboy. Though I'm a tomboy with style." She posed, one hand on her hip and a flirty look on her face.

He tried to imagine her on a horse, but the image failed to materialize.

She held up a hand. "Wait a moment. I'll show you." She walked to one of the bedrooms.

Lost in a cloud, unable to take his eyes away from her, he watched her body sway back and forth gracefully. The door closed with a click and he turned back to the laptop. If he was going to solve her problems, he was going to need his computer with him and her distracting beauty gone. The challenge excited him. He hadn't felt excited in a while.

The bedroom door opened and Kenzie reappeared wearing jeans, a white shirt, red leather cowboy boots and a matching red hat. She posed for him like a runway model. For a moment he thought his heart would stutter to a stop. She walked back and forth, her hips swaying and he couldn't catch his breath. She looked adorable, delectable and so sexy he wanted to kiss her.

"You certainly look the part." What he really wanted to say was that she looked absolutely stunning, but they'd just met and that would be inappropriate.

"Of course I do. I don't play at being a cowgirl. If I'm going to dress like this, I'm going to know how to flaunt it."

She sported the look just fine in his estimation. He felt a huge thud in the area of his heart and for the first time in his life he was willing to fall into lust. Oh, hell, he was going to fall in lust with her.

No. No. He didn't have time to be in…whatever. He still had his life to figure out and her software problem. He went back to contemplating how he would fix her software…or her.

He turned back to the computer. He felt her behind him, the heat of her body like a solar flare. "You're hovering," he said, half turning to glare at her.

"I'm fascinated by what you're doing."

"I'm just playing to see where the glitches are. I don't have my applications here to start working on the fix. I'm going to need your laptop for a couple hours."

"I'll be gone for a couple hours. Take all the time you need."

He nodded and closed the laptop, tucking it under his arm. "You know, I'll have access to everything on your laptop. I'll know all your deepest, darkest secrets." He'd already figured out she had no password protection set up.

She laughed. "Yeah. You're going to find out I play Warhammer."

That surprised him. "So do I." He'd never met a woman who liked adventure gaming.

She tilted her head at him. "We'll have to team up some day. You, me and my brothers. They get pretty intense."

He had the feeling she could best them all.

He walked to the door and she opened it to let him out. She leaned against the edge of the door and gave him a smile that practically melted his insides.

"You're not what I expected."

"What did you expect?" he asked.

"Horn-rimmed glasses, plaid shirt and socially awkward."

His eyebrows rose. Ten years ago he'd been exactly that—horn-rimmed glasses, plaid shirt and socially awkward. Laser surgery corrected his vision, a stylist helped with his wardrobe and experience conquered his awkwardness. He knew he tended to be introspective, but having millions in the bank had made him a target for women who had been throwing themselves at him for years, and he'd become adept at recognizing and avoiding them. "I'm sorry I wasn't what you imagined."

"You're better." She grinned mischievously, a flirting sparkle in her eyes.

Again, he felt a tug on his heart. He didn't know how to respond to that. He liked her directness, but unpredictability lurked behind her dark eyes. He held up the laptop. "Hopefully I'll have this ready for you when you get back from your lesson." Or not. He wondered how long he could drag out fixing her software just so he could be near her. He wanted to be near her.

* * *

Kenzie watched him walk down the hall toward his suite. She really had expected *geek extraordinaire*. The fact that Reed Watson was a very handsome man made her tingle. She wanted to run her hands through his shaggy blond hair and kiss him. She'd never been attracted so strongly to a man on a first meeting.

Not even Sam. He'd worked his way up through the executive ranks at Saks and eventually landed as the director of marketing. They'd had a lovely time over the years, but Sam wasn't into commitment. He'd been quite emphatic about making sure she understood his feelings from the beginning.

Sam had warned her she'd hate Reno and he wasn't giving up his job to follow her. How could she back away from her career for a backwater town when she'd been all over the world and seen the best fashion the world had to offer? He was wrong. In the time she'd been in Reno, she'd come to love it. The town wasn't jaded or as self-important as Vegas. Reno knew what it was and reveled in its frontier-town mentality.

Anything was possible. Look at Miss E., Kenzie's grandmother. She'd taken a classic hotel and casino and made it new again. She'd got her family back together, and no one was unhappy. Hunter and Lydia were having a baby. Nina and Scott would be getting married soon. Donovan and Hendrix were cooking up a storm. Even though she was the odd one out, she was used to being the only girl. Besides, she wasn't ready to settle down.

Her cell phone rang and she went back into her suite to answer it. Rapid French overwhelmed her.

"Slow down, Monique. What is going on?" Monique Benoit designed her own line of casual wear that had grown very popular over the past few years. Kenzie had discovered her and suggested that Saks offer her a contract for her designs. She'd always been able to spot the up-and-coming designers and talk stores into showcasing their lines.

"That woman," Monique snarled. "I hate her."

"What woman?" Kenzie cradled the phone against her ear with her shoulder while she poured herself a glass of iced tea.

"That Anna. The one who replaced you. I cannot work with her. She is an…an imbecile."

"She came highly recommended." Sam had campaigned for the store to hire her, replacing Kenzie. "I'm sorry she's not working out with you."

"She is not you, Kenzie."

"I'm sure she'll work out if you give her some time."

"I don't know," Monique said, her tone resigned. "I like working with you."

"And I with you. Your clothes are selling well here." Kenzie had opened a small store in the hotel spa for Monique's line. "I know it's not like having your lines in Saks, but Reno is growing. I think you should consider expanding your lines with your own stores."

"I think on it, but I'm not ready yet. I have no… worries about you in Reno. It is this Anna I have uncertainties about."

"She'll work out, Monique," Kenzie soothed. "Change requires a period of adjustment. Talk to Sam. I'm sure he'll help."

"Maybe." Monique sounded dispirited.

Kenzie wondered just what Anna was doing that upset Monique so much.

"Come to Reno and play for a week," Kenzie offered. "I'll show you around and we'll explore. There's some great hiking here."

Monique, like Kenzie, was a hiker. She would love the mountain trails, the hot springs in unexpected places and the beautiful vistas.

"I will think on that," Monique said before she hung up.

Kenzie tried not to let her friend's conversation bog her down. Everyone she'd worked with in New York would adjust to the new buyer. She was sure Anna would work out. She might not have Kenzie's intuition about things, but she would learn.

Chapter 2

Maya sat on her horse as though born to the saddle. Kenzie knew how to ride. As a tween she'd been horse-mad and Miss E. had arranged for her to have riding lessons. For a while as a child, Kenzie had thought about being a cowgirl working on a ranch, but fashion won out.

Maya was turning into a little fashion plate all by herself. She wore black jeans, a pink shirt with red fringe and matching pink boots. A pink Stetson sat on her head. She'd wanted a pink saddle, but her mother, Lydia, had said no.

Kenzie watched Maya race her horse around the barrels. Hector Ibarra, her teacher, sat on the fence, his booted feet hooked around the bottom rail. Patti, Hector's daughter and Maya's best friend, sat on her own horse out of the way.

Kenzie wasn't all that interested in barrel racing; she just wanted to bond with her niece.

"Good time," Hector called when Maya finished the course. "You're going to be competition racing in another couple months."

Maya preened, grinning happily. Kenzie remembered being nine years old and loving the attention after doing something right.

Kenzie pulled up to the start line, and when Hector called time she kicked her horse into a gallop and raced around the barrels. Her time was terrible, but she enjoyed herself and knew she'd never be a pro.

After the lesson, Maya and Kenzie walked their horses back to Maya's home.

"I can't wait for my baby brother to be born," Maya said.

"I'm sure your mother feels the same way," Kenzie replied with a laugh. "She's getting kind of tired being pregnant."

"She told me once the baby is born the hard work starts."

Kenzie had absolutely no experience with babies. "When they're first born they just eat, sleep and poop."

"Ick." Maya turned into the driveway leading up to her house. Her dog, asleep on the front porch, came to her feet and trotted down the driveway to greet them.

Kenzie enjoyed Maya's company. In fact, until Maya had come into her life Kenzie had never been around children.

They walked their horses to the barn and dismounted.

"I want Mom and Dad to name the baby Sylvester," Maya said as she unsaddled her horse, draped the saddle over a saddle tree and reached for a brush to groom her horse.

"Sylvester! Sweetie, I don't think that's going to happen." Kenzie unsaddled her horse and started to groom it. "Where did you get a name like Sylvester?"

"In a book. I like the name. I think it sounds noble."

Kenzie shook her head as she groomed her horse. Dust billowed up with each stroke of her brush. The animal's tail swept back and forth and its eyes closed as it relaxed.

"Sylvester is better than plain old Christian." Maya lifted a front hoof and slid a pick under the shoe, cleaning the dirt and mud out. She had to learn to take care of her horse as part of the price of ownership.

"I think Christian sounds like a wonderful name." Maya simply frowned.

They put the horses away in their stalls, made sure they had plenty of fresh water and alfalfa hay in the manger, and headed to the house.

Lydia lay on the sofa in the family room while Hunter puttered about the kitchen grilling chicken. Seeing Hunter so domestic amused Kenzie no end. He'd always been the first one to dare everyone to climb a tree, to vault over a fence or to jump off the roof into the pool. Lydia had tamed him. Kenzie had never seen him so happy.

"Need some help?" she asked.

"Toss the salad," he ordered, pointing at a bottle of dressing.

She did as instructed. He whistled as he brushed a final layer of flavoring on the chicken legs with the special marinade made from their chef brother Donovan's secret recipe. The rising scents of the marinade and the cooked chicken made Kenzie's mouth water. She'd eaten in five-star restaurants all over the world, but they didn't even begin to compare with Donovan's cooking. His fiancé, Hendrix, made such mouth-watering desserts that the hotel couldn't keep anything in stock in the diner and the main restaurant.

"Any signs of a baby yet?" Kenzie put the salad on the dinner table.

Lydia pushed herself to her feet and waddled across the family room to the dining table. "I'm so ready. I don't think I have another three weeks in me."

Hunter laughed. Maya pulled out a chair for her mother. Lydia sat down heavily with a faint groan.

"I hear you met Reed Watson today." Hunter set the platter of chicken in the center of the table and sat down. He forked a chicken leg onto Lydia's plate and then another one onto his. He slid the platter closer to Maya who used her fingers to grab a leg. Lydia frowned, but said nothing.

"He's going to do his magic on my laptop." Kenzie reached for the grilled broccoli and a baked potato.

"He's one of the foremost specialists on internet security in the country. I heard he was asked to lecture at the War College in Rhode Island."

"Miss E. told me that. He's kind of cute, too." Kenzie filled her salad bowl. Heat curled up inside her at the memory of his warm hands and blue eyes. She'd so wanted to push the tangle of blond hair off his forehead she'd had to clasp her hands behind her back.

"And he's single," Lydia put in with an arch look at Kenzie.

"Just because you two lovebirds are still in the

throes of marital bliss doesn't mean I have to be, too. I don't have time for the love mojo. Besides, Scott and Nina are next up in the marriage queue." And then probably Donovan and Hendrix. That was enough marriage for her. She wasn't looking for that special someone in her life. Not after Sam. He'd burned her. He'd hurt her in a way she didn't like to think about. Though the image of Reed hunched over her laptop almost made her sigh.

"I know that face," Hunter said.

"What face?" Kenzie worked to relax the frown.

"The 'I hate dudes' face."

"I don't hate men," Kenzie said. "I just don't like men who think a woman's career is less important than theirs." Or who took credit for ideas not their own. The first time Sam had stolen one of her ideas, he'd been so apologetic she'd forgiven him on the spot. She'd tried to tell herself she loved him and he loved her, but still it seemed that every time she came up with something interesting, somehow it would end up being his idea. Until their last fateful argument.

"You sound like someone hurt you," Lydia said.

Kenzie had confided in Nina, but had not felt as if she'd known Lydia enough to tell her. Now that she'd learned Lydia was a kind, nurturing person who wanted others to be happy Kenzie wanted to unburden her soul, but not now with Maya in the room. Maybe later.

"I was. Now I'm just angry." Kenzie finished her salad and sipped iced tea. She refused to dwell on Sam's betrayal.

"Do you want to talk about it?" Hunter asked curiously.

Kenzie shook her head. "Talking isn't going to do anything."

"It might make you feel a little better."

Kenzie didn't want to feel better. She wanted to feel angry. Anger motivated her. She would show Sam she would be okay.

Later, on her way out to her car, she received a text from Reed. Have some ideas I want to run past you. How about dinner?

She texted back, Just had dinner. How about a drink?

He responded. Eight in the bar.

She agreed. She would have time to shower and change into something else. She enjoyed being a cowgirl, but she didn't want to look like one all the time. And the boots made her feet hot and sweaty. She drove back her thoughts on what she would wear that would made Reed Watson's eyes shine with approval.

Reed waited in the bar, anxious for Kenzie to arrive. He noticed his palms were sweating. It had been a long time since a woman made him sweat. The feeling was exciting as well as disarming. A lot like Kenzie herself. A waitress appeared with a glass of wine. She set a napkin down on the table and then the glass on top of it. The stylized logo of the Casa de Mariposa decorated the center of the napkin. For a moment, he could only stare at it. He owned a casino. He wanted to pinch himself. How had this happened?

A glance around showed the bar was almost full. The chiming of the slot machines outside gave him a thrill. He owned slot machines, a roulette table, a bunch of blackjack tables, and God knew how odd that felt.

He'd met Miss E. when she'd taught a poker class in Las Vegas. He'd been fascinated by her lecture. He'd gone back several times trying to figure out the different odds of the game. Finally she'd started giving him private lessons. And when the poker tournament had come along, he'd been happy to sponsor her, certain she'd win the Casa de Mariposa. Even Lydia, who'd also sponsored her, had been surprised. And now the three of them were co-owners.

The journey from computer genius to casino owner amazed him. What was his next step going to be? He didn't know. His whole train of thought disappeared when Kenzie walked into the bar. His breath caught in his throat. She looked stunning in dark maroon tailored pants and an ivory silk blouse. A gold chain looped around her neck and bounced against her throat as she walked. She'd swept her short hair back from her face. Her very presence lit up the whole bar. He found himself smiling and couldn't seem to stop.

He stood as she slid into the booth. "Good evening."

She smiled at him. "Hi, and good evening to you." She paused as the waitress rushed to the table to take Kenzie's order. She chose a key lime martini, which surprised him. He didn't think she was a martini type of person. "You look like you have good news."

Her statement dimmed his smile. "Not really."

"What do you mean, not really?" She gave a little pout. "That doesn't sound good."

The way she looked at him made him want to slay dragons for her. "Where did you get this software?"

"I hired a company in Canada that came highly recommended." The waitress brought her martini and she took an experimental sip, then nodded at the waitress, who smiled back.

"Well, fixing your program is going to mean pulling it apart down to the core and rebuilding it, module by module."

"That's not good news."

He scrambled in his head trying to make the better news. "The good news is, it's fixable. But it's going to take time."

She frowned at him. "How much time?"

An ache started in his chest. He wanted to be her hero and fix it yesterday. "A few weeks maybe. I won't really know until I get started. I don't know what I'll be able to keep or what will need to be tossed."

"We'll work this out." She took a sip of her martini. "My grandmother can't say enough good things about you."

"She's made me feel like a part of your family."

"Miss E. is good like that. Once you get the Miss E. Seal of Approval, you're in for life with no escape." She chuckled.

He laughed, pretty sure Miss E. wasn't about to let him get away. "I don't want to escape."

"Why did you stake my grandmother for the poker game that resulted in all this?" She held up her hand in a sweeping gesture.

"Because I knew she'd win and…well…" He looked around. "Owning a casino is cooler than owning a yacht or an island. And the only thing cooler than a casino would be owning a hockey team."

"I'm a football fan myself. Owning a casino is way cooler than anything."

He nodded. "It's so hedonistic. It's about potential and luck and energy." He leaned forward, looking her straight in the eye. "This may sound corny, but I like seeing people having fun."

"You sound like you haven't had much fun in your life."

He'd been busy making money. "I'm working on that." He was betting she could help him in that department.

She cupped her chin in her hand. "Having fun shouldn't be work."

He didn't quite know how to respond. "When I started my first company, I had fun. I loved working with computers, I loved creating new software and seeing it fly out into the marketplace. The bigger my company grew, the less fun it became."

She nodded. "So then what did you do?"

"I got out." He'd sold his company for mucho millions and decided now was the time to have fun, only to have his father face cancer. "I devoted a lot of my life to my company and I needed to start devoting my life to me. What about you? Your grandmother is really proud of you and your brothers."

"She's thrilled we're all back in the fold. If I didn't know any better I'd think she's been planning this for years."

A shadow fell across them and Reed glanced up to Hendrix Beausolie with a plate in her hand. "Here." She put the plate down midway between Reed and Kenzie and placed a smaller plate in front of Kenzie and another in front of Reed. "Try this."

Hendrix had recently made headlines with her innovative approach to baking pastries. A glowing article in *Reno Today* magazine had brought her a new fan base. People flocked to the restaurant and diner just to have her brownies. Her recent engagement to Kenzie's brother Donovan had made her a minor celebrity in the family.

"Why are you here so late at night?" Kenzie asked.

"The swing dance contest Donovan and I were going to was canceled, and I've been mulling this dessert over in my mind for days so I thought I'd try it while he's working on his food orders for the week." She shoved into the booth next to Kenzie. "Blueberry white chocolate cheesecake. Try some." She slid a slice onto a small plate and pushed it at Kenzie. She filled a second for Reed and a third slice for herself.

Reed forked a bite into his mouth and let the dessert sit on his tongue for a moment. Hendrix was an amazing pastry chef. The subtle tastes of vanilla, white chocolate and blueberry were heavenly. He devoured the slice in less than a minute.

"Wow," Kenzie said, admiration in her tone. "This is to die for." She forked another bite into her mouth and chewed, a dazed look filling her eyes.

"Yeah." Hendrix grinned. "Scott and Nina decided they didn't want champagne cake for their wedding. So I decided to try this. What do you think?"

"I can't give you an honest opinion until I eat another slice." Kenzie grinned at Hendrix.

Hendrix laughed. "I figured you would." She slid another slice onto Kenzie's plate.

Reed tried to eat healthy, but was willing to overlook his health for the decadence of Hendrix's dessert. He finished the second slice. "I approve."

"You only approve," Hendrix said.

"Right now, I really want to marry you."

She held up her left hand and flashed a brilliant yellow diamond ring. "Taken."

He laughed. "Multimillionaire."

Hendrix tilted her head. "Money means nothing to me."

"That's why I'd marry a woman like you."

"You get me in the next life." She stood up and slid out of the booth.

"Fair enough." He was so comfortable with this family. As an only child, he'd missed having siblings.

Hendrix waved as she headed back toward the kitchen.

"Are you okay?" Kenzie said quietly.

"I'm an only child and I always wanted to have brothers and sisters," he said, a wistful tone in his voice.

"Until one of them decapitates your dolls."

Reed stared at her, shocked. "Your brothers decapitated your dolls?"

"Scott always wanted to play soldier with his G.I. Joes and I wanted to play fashion Barbie. He found a bunch of old G.I. Joes somewhere and exchanged their heads for the Barbie heads and wouldn't tell me where he hid them. He came close to losing his life over that." She burst out laughing. "Though now I do think it was pretty funny. I can't imagine being an only child," Kenzie said.

"I always felt like I was on the outside looking in,"

Reed confessed. "I wonder how my life would have been different if I'd had siblings."

"You'd probably have Barbie heads on all your G.I. Joes. Having siblings means you never got the last biscuit because one brother would lick it to keep it for himself and no one would eat it after that."

"I like your brothers. I don't want to know which one did it."

"All of them," she said with a smile. Her face had gone dreamy with her memories. "Learning to share wasn't a bad skill, but sometimes I wish I could have had just a little bit more time with Miss E. before someone came in with a scraped knee. Though I'll admit, having siblings taught me that life wasn't always about me."

Whatever her memories were, they were happy memories because she kept right on grinning.

"Having your parents' undivided attention has its drawbacks. Someone was always watching. I couldn't get away with anything."

"Your parents kept you honest."

He narrowed his eyes and she squirmed. "What did you do?"

She shrugged. "Nothing big. I stole a pack of gum when I was seven or eight. And I was so consumed with guilt I put it back. I've never told anyone what I did."

A woman with a bit of larceny in her soul—she was damn near perfect. "No one?"

"No one." She pointed her fork at him. "And you're going to keep it that way."

He held up his hand in surrender, but he wondered

what he could get to keep her secret. "I promise to keep your secret."

She burst out laughing. "And you?"

Should he tell her? They were sharing. "Once upon a time, I thought I wanted to be an activist. I broke into the school computer when I was at MIT. For a student there, this was a rite of passage. I didn't want to do any real damage, but I did change one grade where I was only getting a B+ and I know I deserved an A. So I gave myself an A."

"That's your worst!"

What he was going to talk about today. "I know it's not as serious as bubblegum."

"Touché." She sipped her wine for a moment. "You sound like you've had a too-serious life. What do you do for fun?"

He didn't answer right away. Should he tell her? Most people thought his hobby way too frivolous and he seldom shared it with anyone but his trusted friends. Finally, he decided to take the plunge. He wanted this woman to like him and if she accepted his hobby without judging, then he would like her even more. "I collect comic books and graphic novels." He waited, trying not to flinch.

She looked interested and not a bit scornful. "Really? Who's your favorite? I always wanted to be Storm, from the X-Men."

He narrowed his eyes, picturing her as Storm with white hair and eyes. "I've always to be the Flash."

"I can see that. He's a bit of a nerd. Although I tend to respect the born heroes rather than the made ones."

"You're not laughing at me." He was astonished. Every other woman he'd told about his hobby had

put it down. Comic books were for kids, not grown
men. He'd finally learned to keep his hobby hidden.
"That's cool."

"I'm cool. I like to hike."

"Is hiking your hobby?" He'd give nature a go if
he could spend more time with her.

"I just like to be outside. My real hobby is creating and sewing fashion wardrobes for dolls. Did
you know the earliest fashion doll was created in the
1300s for an English Queen who wanted French fash-
ions for her court? She sent a note to Paris asking for
fashion dolls to be sent to her so she could choose a
new wardrobe."

For a second, Reed was amazed. His only acquain-
tance with dolls were the ones found in every retail
store. "It must have been great to be the queen."

"That story got me started collecting fashion dolls
from eighteenth and nineteenth century France."

"Do you play with your dolls?"

She shook her head. "These are antique dolls. Usually, I display them, but they are still packed away
because I haven't time to unpack them. Right now,
I'm sewing a whole wardrobe for Maya's Barbie doll
as a Christmas present. She wants a bridal gown with
bridesmaids' dresses."

"You design clothes, too?"

"I originally planned to go into design, but ended
up in the business end. I can make pretty things, but
nothing innovative."

He doubted that. "I think you're selling yourself
short."

She sat back studying him. "I've spent a lot of time
around designers, established ones and new ones. I've

spent a lot of time around clothes and what American women want to wear. I know my limitations. What I am good at is picking out the hot new trends."

He didn't believe her. She'd already shown her imagination to be boundless. That was incredibly sexy. "I admire that in you."

"Fashion is very personal. Women tend to be judged by what they wear. Women who walk into Walmart in stained, dirty clothes are treated a lot differently than women who walk into Walmart looking like a million bucks. Image is everything."

Her talent was just as important as anyone else's. He understood about image. Steve Jobs wore the same thing every day. Bill Gates still looked like a geek but more fashionable. And for himself…

"What are you thinking so intensely?" Kenzie asked.

"I'm thinking about image. Women aren't the only ones who consider how they look. Albert Einstein had a wardrobe that consisted of two weeks of the same style pants, shirt and sweater because he didn't want to think about clothes. Stephen Hawking dresses in Armani. Angelina Jolie wears a lot of black because she doesn't want to have to think about matching clothes. Even I had to think about my image. I tended to stay out of the public eye, but once my company reached the Fortune 500 list, I was scrutinized for everything. I couldn't go to work anymore with holes in my jeans. I didn't understand for a long time that image was just as important as my product."

"For you, your image is about power," Kenzie replied. "And success and control. If you looked like a slob, analysts would see your company as ill-run and sloppy, that you didn't care about profit and the bottom line. Steve Jobs may have worn the same thing every day, but it was neat, clean and looked like he meant business."

His father had been a naval officer; he cared about projecting power and confidence. Which he did with his pristine uniforms and commanding presence. He always felt he should have been accepted for what he accomplished, not for how he looked.

"You're thinking hard again." She shook her head.

"How do you know?"

She rubbed the space between her perfectly plucked eyebrows. "You get this little crinkly line between your eyes."

Reed shook his head. "When I asked to talk to you about your software program and the problems, I never expected our conversation to veer into such personal territory."

Kenzie reached across the table to take his hand and patted it. "How well do you know Miss E.? Because she would have had all this information about you thirty seconds after she met you. She could get information from a stone."

"No kidding. After five minutes I was ready to show her my report card from first grade." He remembered feeling as if he was under a microscope with the older woman and it made him uncomfortable, but with Kenzie he wanted to tell her things about himself. This was getting stranger by the second. "You are good."

Kenzie grinned. "I learned at the feet of the master."

"Is every conversation with you going to end up being so personal?"

She gave him a sly smile. "If we're going to talk

about the weather, we don't need to personalize it. But we weren't talking about the weather."

He felt his blood race through his body. She was sexy and scary. Revealing so much about himself so easily wasn't in his nature. He'd always been a little reserved. Once he became wealthy people were always at him. They wanted money. They wanted advice, endorsements or to be seen with him. And he just wanted to be normal. He didn't own any real estate except for a small condo in Seattle and his father's home in San Diego. He drove a Lexus, his only vanity, because he liked nice cars. He gave 20 percent of his yearly income to charity. He voted in every election, but stayed away from politics. He didn't want to be a mover or shaker in the world; he simply wanted to be left alone to pursue his own interests.

Kenzie patted his hand. "Stop thinking. What happens happens in its own time. Just stay in the moment. I had a friend who used to say life is what it is, stop tormenting yourself about what life isn't."

Her skin was soft on his and he stopped himself from groaning as his pulse sped up and he suddenly wanted more than just a touch from her. "Easy to say, but not so easy to do," he admitted. "So teach me how to stay in the moment."

"Stop thinking about the past. Stop thinking about every little thing as it happens. Every day is a do-over. Make it count. Do something unexpected."

Do something unexpected. For the first time in his life he gave in to an impulse. He half stood, leaned over the table and kissed her on the mouth. Her lips were soft and silky and her breath tasted of the martini she'd drunk. For a moment, her lips opened under his and then she suddenly drew back and pushed him away, her eyes wide in surprise. As he sat down again, she pressed her fingers to her mouth.

"Is that unexpected enough?"

She slid out of the booth. "I have to go." She turned and half ran out of the bar.

Reed was stunned at his boldness and even more surprised at her response. Was she rejecting him? Of course she was. But there was something about that kiss that stayed with him.

Chapter 3

"And he kissed me," Kenzie said as she bent over the dining table, scissors in hand, cutting out the last piece of the bridal gown she'd designed for Maya's present. The other pieces were stacked in a pile near her elbow. Scattered scraps of lace dotted the table along with satin ribbon, spools of white thread and what she called her super-duper, extra-magical sewing machine.

"You did tell him to do something unexpected." Nina had to be the reasonable one. Her knitting needles clicked. A pair of booties in a silvery white took shape beneath her fingers. Knitting had always been Nina's hobby and she was having a field day knitting for Lydia. She'd already knitted a sweater and hat for baby Russell and had a blanket next on her list.

"I didn't mean right then. Later, after I was long gone."

"He could have kissed any other woman," Nina pointed out calmly, "but he kissed you."

Kenzie was as flustered as she was turned on. His kiss had curled her toes and sent a stab of desire through her so strong she'd been unable to catch her breath for an hour afterward. "He's my grandmother's partner. He co-owns the hotel and casino with her and Lydia."

"So what?" Nina said with a chuckle. "He's still a man and you're a beautiful woman."

Kenzie wanted to stamp her feet and scream. Her best friend wasn't reacting the way Kenzie thought she would. She'd expected Nina to understand her confusion.

"Did you kiss him back?" Nina's voice sounded sly and amused.

"No! Of course not!" She carefully snipped the last bit of fabric and placed the final piece of the gown's skirt with the others.

"Why not?"

Because she'd still be there kissing him if she had. "It's too weird. If I get involved with him, my grandmother will be all up in my business."

"That would distract her from being all up in my business," Nina said ruefully.

"You just want me to throw myself on the 'I'm-your-friend' sword. Not doing it." Kenzie sat on a stool next to Nina. "The real problem is, I liked the kiss." She wanted to kiss him again and again and again while running her hands through his tousled blond hair. She wanted more than just a kiss. Her breasts grew taut and a hunger grew deep in the pit of her stomach.

The real problem was that Reno was her new home and she didn't want complications while she figured out her place. Reed was a complication. She had too many things to do.

Her phone rang, and she answered it, glad for the distraction from Reed.

The boutique manager sounded harried. "We're having a problem with the computer. Again."

"Did you call tech support?"

"Not yet. I will after I hang up."

"I'll be right down." She glanced at Nina, who grinned at her. "What?"

"Nothing."

"I have to go."

"This conversation isn't over." Nina wrapped her knitting around the needles and slipped it in her tote.

"Yippee," Kenzie said as she headed toward the door.

"The computer just went haywire," Bianca Cranston said.

Bianca was a small, round woman with pale brown hair surrounding a heart-shaped face. Though a little on the plump side, she dressed with a flair for showing her curves rather than attempting to hide them. Today she wore a rose-colored blouse over a gray pleated skirt. She'd wound a Hermès scarf around her throat, making the outfit look expensive and chic. Kenzie maintained that even the plainest outfit could be made to look regal with the addition of an expensive silk scarf. She allowed her employees to wear the scarves in the store so customers could see how easily one scarf could add character.

A few seconds after Kenzie arrived, Reed strode into the store. When Kenzie spotted him, her cheeks flamed with heat and her heart skipped a beat. He looked so handsome in black jeans and a black knit polo shirt with his ragged hair curling around his ears. He almost looked like a pirate. All he needed was a gold hoop earring to complete the image.

"What's the problem?" Reed asked, setting a brief-case down on the counter.

Bianca held her hands up. "I was in the middle of a transaction when the computer shut down and the screen went blank. I checked next door at the ski shop and their computer is fine."

"Let me see what I can figure out." He bent over the computer without even the briefest glance at Kenzie.

Kenzie backed away, feeling a little miffed. He acted as though nothing had happened between them. First she wanted to slap him. Then she wanted to kiss him. *Don't go there*, she scolded herself. He'd only been doing what she'd suggested, something unex-pected. Why did she think his kiss meant anything more?

Men. Can't live with them. Can't live without them. They're all idiots.

She stayed out of his way. He opened his briefcase to show rows of tools and a box of CDs. "Do you have something you can use while I'm fixing this?"

"We can use the computer next door to ring up purchases," Kenzie said with a nod at Bianca.

Reed pulled a couple of tools out of the briefcase and opened the side of the computer. In seconds he had parts strewn across the counter. Kenzie found a stool and sat down to watch him.

"Done anything unexpected today?" he asked, a playful tone in his voice.

Kenzie tilted her head. "No. But the day is relatively young yet."

He pinned her with a sexy stare. "Do you want to do something unexpected with me?"

Did she? Yes, but she wasn't going to admit it. "I believe you already did that."

He grinned. "I had something else in mind."

"Such as what?"

"Have you ever gone bowling?"

Not a day in her life. "Bowling?"

"How about tomorrow?"

She took out her phone. "I need to check my schedule."

He took the phone away from her and placed it on the counter. "Don't. Remember, unexpected. Yes or no?"

She studied him for a moment, her mind whirling. He was taking her advice a little too much to heart, but excitement surged through her. "Yes." She could rearrange her schedule easily enough. That came out of her mouth way too easy.

"Good. Meet me tomorrow evening at four thirty by the concierge. I'll even throw in dinner."

"Is this a date?"

He paused as though considering her question. "Maybe this is just me taking your advice."

"Okay." She found she couldn't stop grinning as he went back to fixing the computer. "How long do you think you need to fix this?"

"Not long." He glanced at his watch.

She saw a customer wander into the store and went over to assist her.

Reed watched her go. The computer was actually an easy fix. A memory stick was loose in its housing. All it took was a screwdriver to pry it out and reset it firmly. He rebooted the computer and nodded at Kenzie who gave him a brief smile before turning back to the customer.

He wanted to linger to watch her work, but he had a meeting with Miss E., Lydia and the chief financial officer.

He found his way through the maze of corridors and offices behind the administration area to the conference room. He sat down at the end of the table.

"Glad you're here, Reed," Miss E. said. For such a tiny woman she had a presence that filled the room.

Lydia looked uncomfortable as she squirmed trying to find a position that wouldn't put a strain on the baby or her back. Her face was drawn and tired. She looked ready to burst, but Reed knew she had another week or two before the baby's birth.

Martin deWitt had been CFO for Jasper Biggins, the original owner of the Mariposa. He was a tall, slim, impeccably dressed man with black hair threaded with gray. A small mustache over his lips gave him an air of sophistication as he spread open file folders and tapped his laptop, bringing the screen to life.

"We have a problem," Martin deWitt said.

Miss E. nodded intently. Reed simply waited. The

winning of the hotel and casino had been so unexpected and new he didn't feel like an owner yet.

"Explain the problem," Miss E. urged.

"As you know, to expedite gambling in the casino, customers purchase cash cards, like debit cards or pre-paid credit cards, for a certain amount of money that can be used with the slot machines. The cards keep track of their winnings and any perks they win. A customer buys ten dollars, which is put on the plastic card and entered into the slot machine, and an amount, say a quarter, is deducted from the balance on the card each time the customer places a bet and loses."

Reed nodded. He understood the logistics of slot machines.

Mr. deWitt looked around the conference table. "The system works well enough, but there have been a few complaints over the years. Yesterday, a big complaint was made when a customer purchased a card in the amount of ten thousand dollars and when she went to use it, it was short five hundred dollars."

"Did someone make a mistake?" Lydia asked.

Martin looked troubled. "I think it's more than just a mistake. Most complaints are handled by the floor managers, but this one came to me. Five hundred dollars is a lot of money to lose on a mistake."

"How did we handle it?" Miss E. asked.

"To make up the difference, we gave him a card for five hundred dollars and it came up short twenty-five. "

Which shouldn't have happened. This was a big problem. "What do you think is going on?" Reed turned over the problem in his mind. This could simply be a computer fix, or was the problem something bigger?

"I'm not sure, but I've tried a small experiment. I loaded different amounts onto twenty-four cards and they all came up five percent short. Which means that every time a customer loads money onto a card, it's five percent short. The house is getting the money, but the customer isn't getting what they paid for."

"I don't like this at all," Miss E. said. "The reputation of this hotel could be irreparably damaged."

Reed studied Martin, his mind working furiously. "Do you know how long this has been going on?"

"I've just started looking into it, but after talking to some of the cashiers, I found there have been complaints going on for a couple years, at least. The problem is that no one in the casino, except for several of the croupiers, has been with the hotel longer than a couple years." Martin opened a file and glanced through it. "Most customers only put ten, twenty-five or fifty dollars on a card and probably never notice that the cards are short by five percent. For those who do discover they've been shorted, a complimentary meal takes care of the difference. But five hundred dollars is a whole different matter."

"How do we fix it?" Lydia clenched her hands tightly in front of her, looking worried.

"It could just be a simple glitch in the software," Reed offered, "which can be fixed. The problem would be taking the whole system off-line, which could hurt our bottom line."

"How long do you think it will take?" Miss E. asked.

Reed shook his head. "I could find the error immediately, or it could be weeks. There's a lot of code to go through." Though he could probably write a program that would help him narrow it down.

"We could have some unhappy customers," Lydia said.

Miss E. waved her hand. "We'll give them Hendrix's brownies for free. They'll be fine."

Lydia smiled. "And maybe a free drink. Or a discount coupon for a dinner."

Martin seemed to relax. Reed could tell he'd expected a very different response.

"I'll fix the glitch," Reed said. "There's no need for anyone to panic."

Miss E. stood up. "Then we'll leave this in your very capable hands, Reed."

Not until later, when Reed had returned to his office in the IT department, did he have a thought. If the casino was taking in the full amount, but the cards were short, where was the missing money going? He would need to talk to Martin deWitt again.

The bowling alley was noisy with the sound of bowling balls rolling down the alleys and the thunder of falling pins. In the background Lady Gaga belted out a song. Kenzie had never been in a bowling alley before. All the lanes except for a few at one end were occupied with what appeared to be teams.

"Why bowling?" she asked as she tied the laces of the bowling shoes Reed rented for her.

"I used to hold bowling parties with my employees."

How interesting. He didn't seem like a bowler, but she was learning that there was as much predictable about him as was unpredictable. He was a hot, sexy mystery. One she was longing to get to the bottom of. "Why?"

"So we could bond and work better as a team." He hefted a bowling ball out of its bag. His ball was a fancy dark red with veins of black and white threaded across the surface. It was so highly polished she could see her reflection in it before he dropped it in the ball stand to the left of their lane.

"Are you bonding with me?"

He jiggled his eyebrows. "We're here to have fun."

How he was able to look goofy and seductive at the same time was beyond her. "I thought we would do something that took us out of our comfort zones."

"You've never seen me bowl."

He helped her choose a black ball for herself that fit her grip and she carried it back to their lane. The group next to them erupted into cheers. Kenzie eyed them curiously. They all wore matching shirts with some logo on the front pocket. Bowling shirts did not make much of a fashion statement.

"She bowled a strike," Reed explained.

"A strike?"

"Knocked all the pins down."

Kenzie just nodded. She hitched up her boyfriend jeans and tugged her red tank top into place. If she could ride a camel to the pyramids in Egypt, she could throw a ball down the lane and knock down the pins.

"Stand here," Reed ordered, pointing at a mark on the slick floor. He positioned her hands around the bowling ball. "Now, you're going to swing the ball back like this and take three steps forward. On the last one you're going to slide, like this, and stoop a little." He demonstrated for her. "Then throw the ball when you reach this mark."

She did so, and the ball ended up in the gutter. The ball was much heavier than it looked. Eventually it reached the back of the lane and disappeared. A moment later it reappeared in the ball return, clinking into Reed's ball.

"You get two tries." Reed helped her position her feet again.

She paced forward and threw the ball. It sort of stayed in the middle of the lane and eventually reached the pins, knocking down three. "I'm a bowling rock star," she cried, raising her arms in victory.

Reed laughed. He sat at the scoring console and entered her score. Then he stood and picked up his ball. She studied the way he stood, his feet together, the ball poised in front of him. He stepped forward and threw the ball in an oddly graceful set of motions. His ball slammed down the lane and smacked into the pins. Several fell down.

"You knocked some down," she said, feeling a small thrill of excitement. She was enjoying herself. Who knew bowling could be so much fun. She wanted to knock all the balls down.

His ball came back through the return. He picked the ball up and swung it again. It rolled down the alley and knocked the rest of the pins down.

"That's a spare."

"I think I'm going to enjoy this." She picked up her ball.

They bowled a few frames and while she waited

for her ball to return after her last gutter ball, Reed announced, "It's time for beer and nachos."

She shook her head in surprise. "I haven't had beer and nachos since college."

"Life can't be all salad and smoothies." He walked over to the bar to put in his order.

She tried not to think about the calories. Oh, well, she'd work it off tossing that ball around and maybe hitting a few pins.

"You don't strike me as a bowler," she said after a couple more frames.

"I had to find a way to connect with my employees besides work. Downtime was important. And stress was a big part of the day."

"How did you get into artificial limbs?" Miss E. had told Kenzie about his business.

He lifted a nacho to his lips, cheese dripping on his fingers. He wiped the cheese off with a napkin. "Five years ago Dad lost his leg below the knee in a training exercise and decided to retire from the navy. I'd moved away from writing phone apps to internet security at the time. I remember what he went through, getting his prosthesis to fit correctly. He wanted a leg that looked like a real leg. Later, I started experimenting myself and ended up developing software that took all the measurements needed and crafted a realistic-looking leg that matched the real leg. Watching my dad walk, you'd never know he had a prosthetic leg. And from that I developed other applications for the medical field."

"That's really impressive." He'd made a huge contribution to making people's lives easier. All she'd ever done was try to make women look pretty.

"I did it because I love my dad." For a second he looked sort of sad.

Kenzie wanted to comfort him to take the look away. She realized he'd never said anything about his mother. "Where are your parents?"

"My dad lives in San Diego and my mom was killed in an auto accident seven years ago."

"That sucks," she said. "I didn't mean to say that quite that way."

"You're right. Losing my mom sucks."

Cheers sounded at the other end of the alley. She glanced around. A woman jumped up and down, throwing her hands in the air and whooping. "I did it. I did it," she cried. Her companions clapped and she bowed.

"What do you want? Where do you go from here after you've made a gazillion dollars?"

He studied her thoughtfully. "That's kind of an intense first-date question."

"You said this was a 'maybe,' not a date. You're avoiding an answer."

"I want to see where the day takes me. I don't want a plan. What about you? Where do you want to go in your life?"

"That's kind of an intense first-date question."

He laughed. "You asked first."

"First I thought I wanted my own fashion empire. Now I'm just thrilled being here in Reno with my family. We're all in the same place for the first time since we were kids. We see each other every day and have fun together. I'm about to be an aunt. Who knew a simpler life could be so rewarding." New York was filled with noise and chaos. Reno was so quiet she could hear the crickets at night.

"Have you always been interested in fashion?" he asked.

"Helping women find that perfect outfit that makes them feel like a million bucks. I enjoy watching their faces when they realize how good they look."

"I visited New York once. I never wanted to go back. It's so busy."

Kenzie nodded. "Reno is so calm and quiet. Being with my family is so wonderful. I love having breakfast with my grandmother and hanging with Maya. I have time for the little things I didn't have time for before. I read four books last month. Those four books have been on my to-be-read pile for five years. I thought I was happy living the 'dream' in Manhattan. I had interesting friends, but missed being with my family. Nina and I haven't been in the same room together in years before I came here."

She didn't know when she'd started to be unhappy with her career. The vaguest feelings of disquiet would appear from time to time, but she'd always bury them and get on with the next step because she was leading a glamorous life. Kenzie hadn't realized she'd become so dissatisfied. She'd grown tired of the egotistical, neurotic designers who had tantrums every hour on the hour for no reason, and impatient with cranky, underfed models. She even started to dread getting on an airplane rushing to the next fashion week.

This man was scary. He made her think about things. Things she didn't want to examine too closely. He'd done things that were changing the world, but the world had changed her into something she wasn't certain she liked.

They finished their game. Kenzie turned in her rental shoes and put her ball on the racks along the back wall of the bowling alley.

"Where are we going for dinner?" she asked as he opened the passenger door of his Lexus.

"What do you feel like eating?"

"After beer and nachos, I need some vegetables."

"I think steak and potatoes would be appropriate."

Reed did make her be bad. "Let's live." She buckled her seatbelt. "There's a country-western bar and grill a couple blocks from here. My brother Scott says it has real man food."

"Real man food!"

"You said steak and potatoes. I'm fulfilling your stated desires."

A knowing little smile spread across his lips. "If you insist."

She liked the way the corners of his lips crinkled up and how his eyes twinkled. His sense of adventure delighted her. Sam's sense of adventure had been confined to what happened inside the city limits of New York.

The country-western bar was already hopping. Line dancers covered the dance floor, swaying and dipping to the twangy sounds of Tim McGraw. Peanut shells crackled under their feet. A waitress in a miniskirt, low-cut blouse and leather wrist cuffs dangling with fringe led them to a booth and slapped menus down on the planked table.

He opened his menu and glanced through the offerings. Kenzie couldn't stop watching him. Until he sat down and started to peruse the menu, Kenzie just couldn't picture him in a country-western bar. It was so out of his element. She could imagine him bending over a long line of computers with a microscope set up on a table. In her imagination he wore a lab coat and a shirt with a catchy saying.

Every man she'd dated since college had been as much as a clotheshorse as she was. Reed was so different. He wore expensive clothes more for function rather than fashion. She couldn't believe she was attracted to him.

"You're staring at me."

"Just pondering the mysteries of the universe."

His eyebrows rose. "What? Like string theory?"

"Nothing that complicated. Who are you wearing?"

He gazed at her, a confused look in his blue eyes. "I don't understand."

"Exactly," she stated calmly. "In the last seven years, I've never gone out with a man under either business or romantic circumstances who wasn't as into fashion as I am."

"And that's important...why?"

"In the grand scheme of things, it isn't important. I was testing myself."

"I'm not sure how to answer that."

"You don't have to." She leaned her elbows on the plank table and smiled at him.

The waitress took their beer order. Reed went back to studying the menu.

"You're still staring at me."

"I know. I'm trying to reconcile my past with my present."

"I thought we were living in the moment. Are you saying that if we hadn't been brought together by circumstances, you would never consider going out with me?"

"It's not you, but me. I've changed somehow, and I can't figure out how. Being away from New York and with my family has made me different. I love being back with my family. I'm like I used to be before I got all New York jaded."

"Is that bad or good?"

"I like myself more."

He nodded as though he understood, but she could still see the confusion in his eyes. She didn't quite understand how to tell him that the change in her had made room for new things in her life. And he was one of those new things.

The waitress returned with their beers and took their order. He chose the house special, steak medium rare and baked potato with everything on it. Kenzie, still full of nachos, decided on an Angus burger, medium-well with onion rings. Maybe not so healthy after all; she'd worry about calories tomorrow. And she would have to worry, because Nina had already decided her maid of honor would wear a form-fitting slip dress that wouldn't allow for an extra pound anywhere on her.

"Want to dance while we're waiting for our food?"

"You line-dance?"

"I've been watching. I've got the steps memorized."

"Then let's dance."

They danced until their food came and they settled back into the booth. Reed attacked his steak as though he hadn't already filled up on nachos. Kenzie discovered she wasn't particularly hungry and picked at her food.

"Why did you help my grandmother with the entry fee for the poker tournament? Until she called me with the news she'd won the Mariposa, I didn't even know she wanted to own a casino."

"A lot of reasons," Reed said.

"Give me one."

"I wanted to learn how to play poker. Miss E. was teaching a class at this little out-of-the-way casino in Las Vegas. The moment I met her, I just knew she had something special, some spark of something special that attracted me. Everyone else I know her age was retired, eating dinner at five o'clock in the afternoon and going to bed at eight. She was just…different."

"That she is," Kenzie said with a laugh.

"I see the same enthusiasm in her that I used to see in hungry young interns every summer. I used to pride myself on finding the hungriest interns to work for me. I never looked for the best or the brightest, but the ones who were most persistent. Your grandmother has that hunger in her still. She might be eighty-five, but she's still living. And I wanted to be around her because the only thing left for me in life was to make more money. In my gut, I knew your grandmother would teach me more in a week than I'd ever learn in a year somewhere else."

"Does Miss E. know this about you?" Kenzie asked. She saw her grandmother as more manipulative than energetic, but not in a bad way. Though she did have a zest for life. "You got sucked right on in.

That's what my brothers and I called Miss E.'s Doppler Effect."

"She made me want to be better," Reed said.

"She does that to a lot of people. But not everyone pays attention." Kenzie had had a school friend who Miss E. had warned her to be careful with because her life was spiraling out in a weird direction and Kenzie was being pulled along. Kenzie's friend had decided Miss E. was old and tired and went on her own merry way. But Kenzie had listened to her grandmother. That had been Kenzie's first experience in a friendship that hadn't ended well. Miss E. never quite interfered with the friendship, but Kenzie finally realized her friend had been on a self-directed path to destruction and Kenzie didn't want to get sucked into it. "Miss E. started out as a blackjack dealer. She wanted to be a showgirl, but was too tiny. So she dealt blackjack at the Tropicana. And then she was a pit boss. Even though she was a black woman in a male-dominated town, she got ahead because people always underestimated her. She has this incredible talent for making you want to be the best you can be. And she used that mercilessly."

"Basically, you're saying your grandmother saw me coming."

Kenzie tilted her index finger at him. "Exactly."

He seemed to ponder her comment for a moment. "I'm okay with that. I benefited."

She patted his hand. "Most people usually do."

By the time Reed saw Kenzie back to her suite, she had to fight herself to keep from inviting him in. She so wanted to keep the evening alive. For a second, he looked hopeful, but she simply bade him good night and closed the door.

Chapter 4

Reed studied the computer monitor, trying to concentrate. His thoughts kept reliving his bowling date
with Kenzie. He couldn't get her out of his mind.
She'd shown herself to be a terrible bowler, but she'd
laughed at herself and went right on trying to get the
ball down the lane. He'd loved that she'd been able
to laugh and keep on going. She'd enjoyed every moment and he'd started to understand what she meant
about living in the moment.

He continued scrolling through the code hoping
he'd just spot something that would clue him into why
the debit cards were always 5 percent off. He'd ex-
perimented, loading cards of different amounts, and
they consistently showed 5 percent less than what
had been purchased.

A knock sounded at his door and he yelled enter.

Scott Russell walked in. Scott, as head of security, had an interest in the missing money, too.

"Can you tell me anything yet about the missing money?" Scott sat down.

"First of all…"

Scott held up his hand. "I need you to tell me in words I understand."

"You're a smart man," Reed said with a half smile. "You'll figure it out."

Scott shook his head. "I can drive a Ferrari. You can drive a Ferrari at a high rate of speed, avoiding other drivers on a racetrack, leading the pack and winning. That's the difference in our skill levels."

"Right now, I'm not making any huge leaps yet. I have to unravel all the code and track where this discrepancy is coming from. I'm in the long, boring, complicated part of the investigation." That could take him minutes or days. He had a lot of code to go through.

"I understood every word you said. You made it too easy. I'm going to need a beer after this."

Reed glanced at his watch. "Well, its five o'clock somewhere in the world and we can pretend to be mentally exhausted and go get that beer." He wanted to get to know the Russell family. He found all of them intriguing. Despite having flourishing careers in other fields, each one had happily given up what they were doing to help Miss E. get the casino back on its feet. That impressed Reed, and the fact that Miss E. generated such strong loyalty with her grand-children made him want to be a part of it.

He didn't have this kind of relationship with his own father. His father had spent thirty years in the navy and many of those years away from his family. Even though his father said he was proud of Reed, Reed knew he would never be the rough-and-tumble, sportscentric son his father had really wanted.

The Russell family was so close-knit Reed felt a sense of envy. No matter how diverse their interests, they all came together to support their grandmother.

The bar was partially full when they entered. Reed and Scott found a booth at the back and ordered their beers. The waitress reappeared with their beers and a large bowl of pretzels.

"So," Scott said, opening the conversation, "I heard you and Kenzie had quite the adventure a couple days ago."

Reed tensed. "Is this an interrogation?"

Scott's grin widened. "Do I need to get out my tools of torture?"

Reed had a mental image of being duct-taped in a dirty cell, fighting rats over a scrap of moldy bread. He tried not to shudder. He already knew Kenzie's brothers were very protective of her.

"We went bowling and had dinner at a country-western bar and grill Kenzie said you and your brothers liked. That's all." He was glad he hadn't given in to the impulse to kiss her at the end of the evening when she'd stood in front of the door to her suite looking so hot his whole body vibrated with the need to touch her.

"Did you kiss her?"

Shocked, Reed blurted, "Is that any of your business?"

"You're leaps and bounds better than her old boyfriend. Nobody liked him." Scott took a long sip of his beer and then popped a couple pretzels in his mouth.

"Sam was more interested in having someone who looked good on his arm at a cocktail party. And you have to admit, Kenzie's a good-looking woman."

Reed was afraid to admit to her brother that he agreed. Kenzie was a fine-looking woman and he liked the way she looked on his arm, too. But he also liked that she was smart and charming. She knew she was good-looking, but she also knew that her looks were just a tool. A tool she used to get ahead professionally the same way she used a pen or her laptop.

"Lydia. Nina. Hendrix." Reed shrugged. "I think all men want a good-looking woman on their arms, and you're no different." He worried he might have gone too far.

Scott just grinned. "Yes. My future wife is gorgeous on the outside and just as gorgeous on the inside. You're right. We all want something beautiful in our arms. But we all have a different opinion of what's beautiful. I can tell you that Donovan, Hunter and I are with our ladies for more than their good looks. Sam was always suspect. He didn't seem to appreciate Kenzie's brains. Every idea she ever had always seemed to end up being his."

"And Kenzie didn't object?" Reed couldn't imagine taking someone else's idea and putting his name on it.

"Kenzie thought she was in love and let a lot of things slide."

"But something happened, or she wouldn't be here."

Scott frowned. "You're right. I don't know what happened but I do know that he issued her an ultimatum—him or her family. She chose family."

"Miss E. inspires incredible loyalty." She inspired it in him.

"And she inspires a healthy dose of fear." Scott raised a hand for a second beer. The waitress nodded and headed toward the bar.

Reed chuckled. "I felt that fear, too. So is the interrogation over?"

"If I'd been really interrogating you, I'd have brought Hunter and Donovan along. That would have been fun for us."

Reed tried not to react. The idea of the three of them ganging up on him made him swallow nervously. Knowing they could gang up on him made him feel connected and happy in some odd way. He'd always tried to make his employees feel that they were a part of something bigger than themselves, but he'd never felt that way. Being with Scott and the Russells did. They made him feel as though he was as much a part of the big picture as they were.

Kenzie stood next to the tall, rounded woman who gazed at herself critically in the mirror.

"I don't think yellow is a good color for me," the woman said.

"This yellow is the perfect color for you," Kenzie said honestly. The soft, creamy yellow perfectly accented the woman's beautiful mocha skin and hazel eyes. "And you don't want it to be looser, but more fitted to your body. Flaunt your curves."

The woman frowned at herself. "I don't know."

"You are a beautiful woman, here in Reno to have fun. Start with that. You have the best asset."

"What asset?"

"Cleavage. Boys love ta tas," Kenzie stated firmly. "I have just the right statement necklace and earrings to add a bit of color. With the right purse and shoes, you'll knock 'em all dead. Now stand up straight. You own the world."

The woman gazed at Kenzie with disbelief.

"And start believing in yourself," Kenzie added as she rushed off to find the shoes and purse she'd already decided the woman needed.

Nina walked into the store as Kenzie was finishing the sale. She perched on a stool. "What do you want for lunch?"

Kenzie thought for a moment. "Anyplace but here."

"Why? Hendrix just brought in a new batch of double chocolate fudge brownies."

"We can take brownies with us. I need to get away."

Nina studied Kenzie for a second. "Okay, how about that new Mexican restaurant down the street? They have terrific empanadas. And the advantage is we can walk."

"Sounds good." Kenzie waited until her assistant returned from lunch and checked in, then grabbed a sweater. The day was cooler than normal, a hint that winter was on its way.

The walk was pleasant. Kenzie listened to Nina talk about her upcoming wedding. By the time they slid into a booth in the restaurant and the waitress handed them menus, Nina was talked out.

"So what's wrong?" Nina asked.

Kenzie sighed. "What isn't wrong?"

"This doesn't sound good. I think we need a round of margaritas."

"It's only two in the afternoon."

Nina shook her head. "Pretend we're in Paris. It's dinnertime there."

Kenzie signaled the waitress to put in their order. "I had a great time with Reed. He took me bowling."

"Bowling?" Nina's eyebrows rose in surprise.

"I'm not quite sure if it was a friend date, a first date or something else."

"The first time Sam took you on a date was to the Metropolitan Museum of Art's annual gala and he tried to talk you into wearing that hideous feathered headpiece." Nina ran her finger down the menu trying to decide what to eat.

"What are you trying to say?" Kenzie asked curiously.

"I'm not sure." She thought for a moment. "Did you have a good time?"

"I had a great time. I think I scored a total of twenty points, maybe it was thirty, but I enjoyed myself and Reed is funny and smart and so different from what I originally imagined him to be." The memory of their bowling date was never far from her mind. She would be thinking about one thing and suddenly she'd relive herself getting all excited at knocking down three whole pins at once instead of another gutter ball.

"What did you think he was?"

Kenzie sighed again. "A geeky, World-of-Warcraft-playing, not-knowing-who-Michael-Kors-is kind of guy?"

"And he isn't?"

"He is, but it doesn't seem to matter as much as I thought it would. I sound shallow, don't I?"

"Of course not, my deep-as-a-puddle friend."

The waitress brought their margaritas. Kenzie took a sip. A bit too salty, but still good. "I feel so awkward around him. He's sort of my boss."

"*Sort of* doesn't mean he is."

Kenzie took another sip. She wasn't certain how to explain herself. "You worked with Carl after you were married and that didn't work out."

"In Carl's mind everyone worked for him. And that is probably the answer to your next question. What was it like?"

"I can tell you Reed is pretty low maintenance." Especially after Sam who never left his apartment without making certain every hair was artistically placed. Kenzie tried to remember what had caused her to be attracted to Sam, if she'd ever been.

"You've only been on one date with him. How can you tell?" Nina licked the salt from the edge of her glass.

"I just can. I've never worked for Scott or Donovan. But I can tell what kind of people they are. Scott's all business and Donovan rules his kitchen with an iron fist."

"Hendrix knows how to handle Donovan," Nina said. "And she handles him brilliantly. In fact, he doesn't have a clue."

"What about you and Scott?"

"I handle him brilliantly, too. And Lydia has Hunter wrapped around her tiny little finger and he's grateful. Why are you worried about Reed?"

Kenzie pondered her answer. "I enjoy his company far more than I probably should for someone I work for."

"Are you worried about a conflict of interest?"

"Look at how my relationship ended with Sam."

"Sam was a douche," Nina said. "He used you."

"Nina, language." Kenzie almost burst into laughter. Hearing her brother's words coming out of Nina's mouth was such a surprise.

"I have five brothers, remember. And Scott is unleashing my inner potty mouth."

"Unfortunately, you're right." Thinking about Sam brought back some of the hurt. Knowing that he used her still stung. "How come you never said anything?"

"I knew you'd figure Sam out eventually."

Sam knew how to act, dress and talk. Kenzie had been in awe of him from the first time she'd met him. He'd exuded power and sophistication. She'd felt honored someone like him would even deign to notice someone like her. "I don't know why I wasted so much time with him."

Nina's eyebrows rose. "He looked good at a cocktail party."

"What do you mean?"

"He was a great cocktail dress that was terribly uncomfortable to put on."

"It's always about clothes with you, Nina."

"I'm not ashamed to say, I'm deep like a puddle." Nina laughed. "And you should talk."

Kenzie shrugged. "I guess I'm a little hesitant about jumping into a new relationship." Sam hadn't been all bad, but his ultimatum to choose between him and her family didn't sit well with her. Then he'd accused her of being too selfish for her own good. When she thought about everything she'd done to further his career, she realized he would never be the person she thought he would be.

She wasn't ready to tell Nina about their last, vicious argument over her future. Nina would have made it her life's mission to ruin Sam and had the power to do so. Nina played Hollywood hardball. Sam would never have been able to stand up against her.

"Take your time. You don't have to rush into anything. Reed is nice. He has a good head on his shoulders and a good heart. He has vision. Your grandmother trusts him and I need nothing else to recommend him as a human being."

Kenzie hadn't thought about that. Having Nina in the same state at the same time with her was just what she needed. "I love being able to talk to you like this. I feel like we're back in college."

"Except we're better dressed, have more money and can have cocktails any time we want."

Kenzie hadn't solved the problem about her feelings for Reed, but she did realize she liked him a lot. And Nina was right, she didn't have to rush into anything.

When she returned to the boutique she found Reed waiting for her.

"I'd like to show you some of the improvements I've made for your fashion software," he said.

"Good. Let's take a look." She'd had no doubt he'd solve the problem for her.

"I thought maybe over dinner tonight."

Kenzie's eyebrows rose, but she forced herself not to shout yes. She just wanted to spend more time with him. "Are you holding my software for ransom?" He looked kind of sweet as he gazed at her, trying to look innocent while being devious.

"Maybe. You did say live in the moment."

Kenzie's eyes narrowed. "Where do you want to go?"

"Maya says the circus acts at Circus Circus are fun."

That sounded like mindless, crazy fun. She was all in. "I haven't been to a circus since I was a kid." Miss E. had taken them every couple of years. She always wondered what Miss E. would have done if she'd run away to join the circus the way she had wanted to on her eighth birthday.

"Then it's a date." He looked hopeful, his beautiful blue eyes searching her face as though expecting her to say no.

"Yes. I'd love to go. Do you think we should invite Maya?"

He looked doubtful. "I thought…well…if you want to invite Maya, let's invite her. But Lydia is three minutes away from delivery and Maya was promised she could hold her baby brother right away."

"Good point. We don't want Maya to have to decide between seeing her baby brother or watching dancing dogs."

He looked relieved and Kenzie couldn't help the amusement she felt. Maya had already seen all the acts at Circus Circus. "We have a date."

He grinned. "I'll meet you at the concierge's desk at…" He looked at his watch. "Around six thirty."

"Why don't you meet me in my suite at five thirty, and we'll have a drink before we go."

He looked startled. "Okay."

She couldn't take her eyes off him as he left the

store. He paused briefly at the door and glanced back at her. She smiled. He waved and was gone.

Promptly at five thirty, Reed knocked at Kenzie's door. In one hand he held a small, stuffed lion. In the other he held a small bouquet of flowers.

His father had been a practical man and considered the circus a frivolous expense. Reed had never been to one and he was excited to be going for the first time with Kenzie.

He liked her and felt comfortable around her. She made him feel at ease. All the women who'd thrown themselves at him over the years always made him feel like prey. They'd tracked him down wherever he was, flirted with him and tried to seduce him. Two had even proposed to him, thinking he'd be intrigued by their boldness. He'd been appalled. Each woman had spent less than ten minutes in his company and told him they were madly in love with him when he knew they were madly in love with his money.

Kenzie opened the door. She wore red skinny jeans, black stiletto heels, and a matching black camisole. Dangling gold earrings decorated her ears and a large gold link necklace nestled in the hollow between her breasts. She was breathtaking. He swallowed hard trying not to look at her breasts.

She laughed as she took the flowers from him. "What's with the stuffed lion?"

"So you can tame the savage beast."

"Are you flirting with me?" she asked as she took the lion and cuddled it against her breasts.

He would give anything to be that lion right now.

That fact that he was indeed flirting shocked him. What was he thinking?

He stepped into the entryway. Her suite was exactly like his except for the small personal touches she'd added. Colorful porcelain bowls decorated the sideboard. She'd changed around the seating and added colorful pillows to the bland beige sofa and matching chairs. The art on the walls looked like something she'd choose. Lots of color and abstract elements rather than the bland landscapes in his own suite.

Two wineglasses sat on the coffee table with a bottle of white wine chilling in a bucket. Condensation dripped down the side of the wine bucket.

She opened a cabinet in the kitchen and pulled out a vase, filling it with water and arranging the flowers in it. She set the vase on the dining table.

"Thank you for the flowers and the lion. No one has given me a stuffed animal since I was a kid."

"There's something really kid-like about going to the circus."

"Haven't you ever been to the circus?"

"No," he said. "My dad was career military and we had man fun."

"Hunting, fishing and sporting events?"

"Something like that," he acknowledged. He loved his father, but his dad had really strong ideas about how to bring up a boy. Though he'd been disappointed when Reed chose not to follow three generations of tradition and join the navy, he'd gotten over it when Reed had made his first million and paid off his dad's house.

She poured a glass of wine and held it out to him.

He sipped the fruity wine and started to relax. After pouring a glass for herself, she sat down next to him. "What else haven't you done that you'd like to do?"

"Once I strike the circus off my list, I think I want to fly in a hot air balloon."

She suddenly grinned. "And you're in luck. The Great Reno Balloon Race is this weekend. What fun. I think you can ride in a balloon."

"I know. That is what inspired me."

"Are we in?"

"Yeah," he answered.

Kenzie's phone rang. She glanced at it. "I think I have to take this. It's Hunter."

"Answer it," Reed urged. He knew the whole family was on edge with Lydia's delivery ready to happen.

She answered and a smile grew. When she hung up, her eyes sparkled. "Lydia went into labor. They're leaving for the hospital right now. I have to call everyone. I'm the designated caller for this event." She jumped up, anticipation on her face as she scrolled through her phone.

By the time she'd called everyone, Reed could feel the excitement filling the room. "What's the plan?"

"Scott will drop Maya off with Miss E. The rest of us will converge here in my suite to wait by the phone for the final word. Babies take a while. Once we have the word, we're all heading to the hospital."

"Don't you think descending on Lydia so quickly will be difficult for her? She'll be tired and probably uncomfortable."

Kenzie took another sip of her wine. "You don't know this family yet. We do not let events like this go unattended. The hospital is only ten minutes away.

We'll be in and out in no time. Besides, Maya was promised she'd have first chance to hold the baby before anyone else in the family except her mom and Hunter."

"We're in for a long night." Reed allowed her to refill his wineglass.

"I'll call down to the kitchen and order dinner. I'm sorry. We can go to Circus Circus any time."

Donovan and Hendrix were the first to arrive. Donovan pushed a cart into the suite. Following him were Scott and Nina. Miss E. and Maya arrived last. While Donovan uncovered dishes and set up a feast on the dining table, Hendrix arranged brownies, cookies and cupcakes on a large platter. Maya bounced back and forth, too excited to sit down. One moment she'd be chattering away and the next she'd burst into song and dance around the room.

"This is so exciting," Nina said. "I can't wait to have my own baby."

"What?" Kenzie said. "Let me quote the great Nina Torres after our biology final. 'It took me years to get this body. There will be no babies.'"

Nina glanced at Scott. "That was before I met your brother." She paused. "Yeah, that's the answer I'm going to stick with."

"Right," Kenzie said.

"You agreed with me," Nina replied.

"I was protecting myself."

Nina burst into laughter. Scott lit a fire in the fireplace while Donovan uncorked two more bottles of wine. Hendrix set up a buffet line on the kitchen island.

Reed sat back and watched everyone. He felt like an outsider again. He'd never had friends like this and seeing the comfortable exchanges between the siblings made him feel as though he were imposing. He watched Kenzie take a plate and start filling it with food.

He stood. "I think I should leave." He wondered if he could steal a couple brownies to stave off his hunger.

"Excuse me," Kenzie said, looking startled. "You're not leaving."

"This is a family moment." His own family moments were few and far between. Even more rare after his mother died.

Kenzie stared at him, her gorgeous mouth partially open. She handed him the plate of food and pointed to a chair. "And you're a part of this family. Sit down, drink your wine and eat your dinner."

Chapter 5

Christian Mark Russell was born two minutes after 7 p.m. Miss E. delegated Kenzie as a driver to transport her and Maya to the hospital. By 8 p.m. Maya hugged the tiny bundle to her chest while Lydia lay on the bed with her eyes closed. Hunter hovered over her, but couldn't take his eyes off his new son. And Miss E. sat on a chair looking astonished that she was now a great-grandmother.

The room was larger than Kenzie expected, with a soothing pale blue paint on the walls and a duck wallpaper border near the ceiling. Lydia lay with her knees draped over a pillow, her face lined with exhaustion. She looked peaceful. Against one wall was a sink and cabinets. Another wall held a sofa that pulled out into a bed, allowing Hunter to spend the night if he wished. Between the bed and sofa was a small bassinet for the baby.

A nurse stuck her head around the edge of the door. "Visiting hours end at 9 p.m. sharp."

Kenzie nodded. She wasn't certain she would be able to pry the baby away from Maya, or Miss E., who watched the little man with such pride. He'd been dressed in a plain white shirt, long sleeves with mittens at the end folding over his hands, a diaper with blue bears on it and a blanket tucked tight around him. Kenzie had never really thought about having children. As the youngest, she'd had no experience with babies.

"Isn't he just perfect?" Hunter said, awe deep in his voice.

"And to think you made him," Kenzie replied, still astonished that her beloved oldest brother was now a daddy. "When I think about babies it's sort of in some abstract way." But up close and personal made her arms ache.

"I never really thought about babies, except you. You were cranky and fussy and wet. You were noisy and smelled bad."

Kenzie elbowed him. "I did not smell bad."

"Kenzie was a sweet baby," Miss E. put in. Maya had reluctantly given up Christian to Miss E. and she cradled the tiny body to her. "And Christian is going to be a sweet baby. And from time to time babies will be cranky and fussy and smell bad. Even Christian."

Lydia chuckled. Though she looked exhausted, her eyes shone with pride.

Christian yawned and let out a tiny sound. Kenzie reached out to touch the smooth cheek. He twisted his head around, his tiny mouth opening.

Kenzie had never thought about having a baby

with Sam. He thought a baby was an app to put on his smartphone. And as long as whatever she wanted didn't ruin her figure, he was okay with it.

Miss E. transferred the newborn to Kenzie, who held him awkwardly for moment. She imagined lying in bed with a baby and Reed leaning over her. Wait! Where did that come from? What was she thinking? She'd barely known him five minutes and she didn't even know yet if he was relationship material, much less daddy material. Abruptly, she handed the baby to Hunter.

"Are you okay?" Hunter asked as he gently transferred his son back to Lydia's waiting arms.

"Why wouldn't I be okay?" Even to Kenzie, her voice sounded defensive. "I'm fine. Really." She couldn't help herself from thinking about Reed. Wondering what kind of father he would be.

"You have this look on your face of sheer, unadulterated panic and you were holding my son."

Miss E. laughed knowingly. "Your sister is thinking about things."

"I'm not thinking about anything," Kenzie replied.

Miss E. gave her a shrewd smile. "Right."

"I think we should just leave," Kenzie said, eager to just be gone. Her thoughts were too disturbing and she didn't like the direction they were going.

"No, not yet," Maya objected.

Lydia leaned over to kiss Maya on the cheek. "He'll be here tomorrow. He's not going anywhere."

"But…but," Maya said.

"Your mother needs to rest." Miss E. took Maya by the hand and led her out the door. Kenzie followed. Again she imagined herself in the bed holding her own baby with Reed right next to her. She shook the image away. She didn't have time for babies. She had a full life and she liked it exactly the way it was. She was happy. Yet a tiny thought lingered at the back of her mind that she could be happy with a baby. Miss E. had always told her that if she wanted something bad enough, she'd find a way to make it work.

She argued with herself all the way back to the hotel. By the time she pulled into the parking lot she'd convinced herself she didn't have the time for a husband and family. As she unlocked the door to her suite, she'd convinced herself that as much as she liked Reed, they had no future of any kind. She was content with her life and had no plans to change.

Reed sat in front of his computer slowly scanning though the long lines of code. The problem of the short-changed cash cards for the casino stayed front and center in his mind as long as he didn't think about Kenzie. Yet he couldn't stop thinking about her. Every time he forced himself to focus on the problem at hand, something would distract him and his thoughts would drift back to her.

She didn't talk about money or expect glitzy things from him. She'd been delighted with the flowers he'd brought and not once took him to task because he hadn't splurged on roses or some other exotic flower. She'd accepted his offer of flowers with a gracious delight that left him wanting to be with her more and more.

Early in his career, he'd been caught off guard by the beautiful women chasing after him. He'd dated them, but the more they expected expensive, extravagant gifts or trips to Paris, the more he started to distance himself until he'd stopped dating almost completely. One woman had even gone so far as to ask him on their second date for a DNA test to see if the combination of their genes would generate beautiful children. He'd dropped her so fast he thought she was still spinning in place. One tabloid had even named him one of the most elusive bachelors in the world.

Kenzie was different. When she looked at him, she saw him for who he was. Not just a wealthy man, but a man. She wanted to have fun with no strings attached. Though she didn't seem particularly interested in him, he found himself growing more interested in her. He liked being with her. She didn't ask him why he drove a Lexus rather than a Mercedes. She didn't ask him why he didn't wear Ralph Lauren or have a Rolex. She didn't ask him about his portfolio or what it was worth. She didn't question him about what he was, but about who he was. He didn't have the answers since he wasn't certain who he was yet.

A knock on his door revealed Donovan pushing a cart into his office, Scott following behind. Heavenly smells accompanied the tray.

"You haven't eaten all day," Scott said, "so I brought you an early dinner."

Reed glanced at his watch. "Since it's barely afternoon, wouldn't it be a late lunch?"

"Details." Donovan uncovered three plates, the scents of a medium-rare filet, white asparagus on a bed of wild rice and coffee tickling Reed's nose.

Scott leaned over Reed's shoulder. "Have you found anything of interest?"

"Not really. Just lots of lines of code, and so far nothing sticks out. This could take a while." Reed reached for a fork and knife. Until this moment, he hadn't realized how hungry he was. He could go for days without eating, especially when confronted with a challenging problem. And a problem this enormous wasn't going to be easily solved. He wished he could speak to the company that developed the software, but it had long since been out of business and he'd been unable to track the head developers.

"I did figure out the money is being siphoned off, but I haven't been able to track where it's going."

Scott took a chair at the conference table and uncovered a plate of brownies. He took one and bit into it. "That's a start. If you can trace where the money is going I can put my contacts on it and find out who's at the receiving end."

Donovan sat down. "I can't help thinking that the health department issues, the construction problems and the security issues are all related in some way."

"I see the patterns, too." Scott pulled out his notebook. He'd told Reed he'd been documenting all the odd things that had been happening over the past two months, which prompted Reed to do the same.

"You're not the only paranoid person in this place," Donovan said.

"Paranoia has kept me alive," Scott offered.

"I'm not particularly paranoid, but the hotel and casino have too many irregularities that keep cropping up and shouldn't be a problem. But they are." Reed opened his own notebook and stared at it. His mind created patterns out of chaos.

"There are fail-safes in place designed to prevent these things from happening," Scott added.

"Then why are they happening?"

"I don't know. but there is no such thing as being lucky or unlucky. Someone is driving these events."

"But you've been able to explain the problems away when you identified the people behind them," Reed said, still squinting at his notebook.

"I think we have some kind of conspiracy going on," Scott added with a frown. "We've been able to catch the visible people, but not the invisible ones."

"Paranoia," Reed said.

Scott shook his head. "Not paranoia. Someone who is pulling strings has intimate knowledge of how the casino and hotel operate. If we can narrow down our suspect pool, I can use my sources to find out who is doing this."

"I'd better get back to work," Reed said.

"Not until you've eaten something." Donovan shoved Reed's laptop aside and pushed the plate in front of him. "Eat."

Reed smiled. "Thanks, Mom."

After their aborted attempt to go to Circus Circus, Kenzie was happy to go to the balloon races. She didn't expect to have the events start at four thirty in the morning. Despite the early hour, she and Reed stood in the chill to watch the Dawn Patrol. Lighted balloons dotted the dark sky like beacons, bobbing in the air, their colors starkly bright against the blackness. The sight was so beautiful that she felt tears in her eyes.

As the sun peeked over the horizon, classic planes

flew over the field in formation while the national anthem blasted out over the loud speakers. The huge crowd hushed.

Reed held out a huge cup of coffee for Kenzie who took it greedily. "Thank you," she said between gulps.

"It's cold." He held his own cup of coffee with both hands.

"When we decided to attend, I expected events to start at a civilized hour...like 10 a.m." She drank more coffee, needing the caffeine.

"I hate when the world doesn't run on my time," Reed said with a chuckle.

His grin widened.

Kenzie felt a wild lurch in the region around her heart. He looked so boyish with the mischievous grin. Again, the urge to push his hair out of his eyes made her half raise her hand. A strange feeling surged through her.

This man was doing something to her. She didn't know what, but she felt so odd, so light-hearted and so happy. Yes, he made her happy. Sam had never made her feel happy like this. She sipped her coffee, trying to analyze what she was feeling and why.

They wandered around the enormous field where the huge, hot-air balloons were still tethered, waiting for their start time. Ascension was at six forty-five. Dawn was still peeking over the horizon and the colorful balloons were so majestic Kenzie was awed.

"I don't think I've ever seen a balloon shaped like Darth Vader's head." Reed pointed at a balloon in midfield.

"How does that make you feel?" she asked curiously.

He started humming the *Star Wars* theme. "I want to run home and get my lightsaber."

"I want to stick cinnamon buns on the side of my head." She cupped her ears. "Look, there's a Smokey the Bear balloon." The balloon, tethered to the ground, swayed gently in the morning breeze.

In a deep, growling voice, Reed said, "And only you can prevent wild fires."

She shook her head laughing. "You spent way too much time watching TV when you were a child."

Reed laughed, sounding a little embarrassed. "I feel as though I should deny that accusation. I was really more into comic books."

Did he just nerd out on her? What the hell. She liked him just fine.

"I remember," she said.

Throngs of people surrounded them as they found a spot to watch the ascension. Somewhere a loud noise sounded and after a few moments, balloons started to ascend into the morning sky.

Kenzie watched, entranced. "That is so beautiful."

Reed nodded as his gaze followed several colorful balloons rising up. Sharing this moment with him was incredible. He slipped his hand over hers. Kenzie glanced at him, startled. His hand curled around hers, warm against the morning chill. She leaned against him, savoring his warmth.

Despite the rockiness of her romance with Sam, she'd never felt so tingly and comfortable and excited with him as she did with Reed. Reed confused her. His kindness and thoughtfulness made her rethink her views on marriage. Lydia's new baby made her rethink her feelings on family. Suddenly, she didn't want to be alone. She wanted something more than just a career. She wasn't quite certain what she wanted, but she wanted it with Reed. That thought gave her pause. She glanced at him.

Reed's face was alight with wonder as he watched the balloons ascend toward the morning sky, the sun casting brilliant light over them. All the colors brought her back to her thoughts about her own line of clothes. She wanted to design clothes in these vibrant colors for women in all shapes. Maybe it was time to rethink that dream.

"This is so amazing." Reed slid an arm around her shoulders. "The hot air balloons in these different colors going up so high make me want to be up there, too."

"Yeah," she replied. "Me, too. It makes me think of all the possibilities." The cares of her world fell away a little bit as she imagined being up so high in the sky, dangling from the tiny gondolas, watching the world become small. The idea was both powerful and scary.

The balloons floated away growing small in the distance.

"We can take a ride in one." Reed gestured at a couple of balloons at the very edge of the field.

"You mean fly away?"

"Not exactly, just kind of up and then down again."

"Okay."

Reed led the way to an area off to the side of the park where a number of balloons hovered, anchored to the ground by thick ropes. Some were already ascending; others waited for passengers. He paid the fee for them and a man helped them climb into the gondola. Inside the gondola, the pilot grinned at them. Behind him were several large cylinders and a burner.

"Ready for your ride?" he asked.

Kenzie nodded. The pilot turned to the burner as a man outside detached all the ropes but one tether. She gripped the edge of the wicker basket, half terrified, half awed as the balloon slowly ascended into the air. Reed held on to her, but a glance at him told him he was just as awed.

"This is amazing," Reed said as the ground receded farther and farther.

"Everything is so small," Kenzie replied.

A gust of wind caught them and the gondola swayed. Kenzie clutched at Reed. His arm slipped around her, steadying her.

As they rose higher, Kenzie said, "This is so beautiful. Thank you for sharing it with me."

"You're beautiful." Reed kissed her, not the delicate first kiss he'd given her, but a more searching one, more passionate and filled with promise.

She caressed his cheek, her thoughts in turmoil. She leaned against him, her head on his shoulder, and let all her cares drop away. This one moment was filled with promise and she wanted to savor it.

They stood, arms around each other as the balloon started to descend. As they stepped out of the gondola, an unusual shyness crept over Kenzie. She didn't know what to say or how to act. Reed studied her cautiously as though expecting to be rejected.

"I apologize," Reed said, "it was wrong of me to take advantage of the moment..."

"Stop." She held up her hand. "Stop. This was the

most wonderful moment in my life. I want more. I want more with you."

"I want more with you, as well." He leaned toward her, brushing his lips across her forehead.

Chapter 6

Reed sat on the sofa in Miss E.'s RV. She moved about the small galley, heating water on the stove. A floral teapot sat on the counter with two delicate matching teacups. In the couple of years he'd known Miss E., he'd learned she loved making a fuss over other people. Tea was a ritual with her.

She put cookies on a plate and set the plate at his elbow on the side table. Then she poured the boiling water into the teapot, waited a few minutes, then filled the teacups and handed one to him. She added sugar and cream to her tea. He preferred his without extras.

"You look troubled, Reed," she said as she settled herself in her favorite recliner. "What's on your mind?"

He wasn't certain how to broach the subject of his feelings for Kenzie. Miss E. was a good friend and somehow, kissing her granddaughter seemed inappropriate. He sipped his tea as he gathered his thoughts.

"I'm not making any headway in the discrepancies with the money cards used in the casino. The person who wrote the software was brilliant and finding the one line of code that…"

"You're babbling, Reed."

He paused. "I am, aren't I?"

"Tell me what's wrong and I know it's not the money."

He fell silent for a few moments, trying to figure out what to say. "I like Kenzie," he finally blurted out.

"Of course you do. She's very likeable," Miss E. replied.

"You misunderstand me. I…really…really…like Kenzie. More than I should."

"What do you mean by 'more than you should'?"

"She's your granddaughter."

"This isn't a problem with her…skin not being paler."

He stared at her, aghast. "I don't care about that. I'm talking about how beautiful she is, how adventurous." How beautiful. How carefree. He wanted more than kisses, he wanted… His thoughts shied away from what he wanted. After all, he was talking to her grandmother.

"I'm her grandmother. I'm not sure I want to know how adventurous my granddaughter is."

He stopped, jolted, aware that his thoughts about Kenzie were anything but chaste. He'd been dreaming about her a lot and those dreams were hot and sensual and each morning when he woke his whole body ached for her.

Miss E. burst out into laughter. "That is an inappropriate facial expression if I've ever seen one."

"What?" He touched his face.

"You had this grin on your face. I can see you like her in that very special way."

From the tiny smile on her lips, he could tell Miss E. was playing with him. "You're enjoying this, aren't you?"

"Every second," she replied, leaning back and taking a sip of her tea. "Have a cookie and tell me what's going on."

"Are you okay with me dating Kenzie?" Not that he and Kenzie were an item yet, but he was planning. His plan included a lot of hope, and going after what he wanted was the way he worked out a problem. He'd never worked out a campaign to woo a woman before. Kenzie was going to take a lot of preparation.

"Why wouldn't I be?"

"Because technically I'm her boss, you're my friend and her brothers could beat the crap out of me. Those are just a few issues off the top of my head."

"I don't know why you're talking to me. Shouldn't you be talking to Kenzie?"

"I'm a detail person, although I'm trying to loosen up." He jammed a cookie in his mouth before he could say more than he wanted. Having Miss E. know he desired her granddaughter made him uncomfortable.

"Stop that. Go with your gut. Throw everything to the wind and enjoy. Gamble a little. Kenzie's special, if I may say so myself. If you have feelings for her, stop talking to me and do something about it." She stood, took his teacup away from him, and opened the door to the RV. "Get out of here. Go get what you want and stop trying to think it through. Falling in love isn't like writing software. Falling in love is about discovery, about the journey. Get started on your journey, Reed, and stop analyzing it to death."

"I'm trying."

"And don't be Sam."

"Sam?"

"Her ex."

"I have no idea how this Sam was with Kenzie."

Miss E. sipped her tea for a moment. "Be yourself. Be spontaneous and don't insist on doing things your way."

"This Sam doesn't sound like he liked Kenzie very much."

"He liked her just fine. But he liked himself more. Now..." She pointed at the door. "Go out there and do what you do."

Reed left, walking back to the hotel. Miss E. had just given him her version of the golden ticket. He couldn't wait to find Kenzie and get started on his campaign.

The bridal boutique was well lit and overflowing with racks of bridal gowns and dresses for the bridesmaid and mother of the bride. Rows of white gowns were bracketed by rows of bright jewel-tone colors and more rows of pastels.

A number of women browsed the shop with older women who were probably their mothers. Grace Torres, Nina's mother, frowned at a rack of pastel dresses with the sign "Mother of the Bride" hanging over them. Kenzie tried to imagine Grace wearing one of the insipid pastel dresses and couldn't.

Grace's personality was too big, too infectious for her to put her dainty size-ten body into one of those too-frilly dresses.

Nina stood in front of five dresses hanging from hooks around the spacious dressing room. She had insisted she didn't have time to try on dresses, but Grace had swooped down on her and dragged her to the bridal salon. Few people could resist Grace Torres when she was on a mission.

"They all look…average." Nina stepped back, eyeing the gowns with a critical look.

"We're supporting local businesses," Grace said. "I think I like this one."

"I want to support local businesses," Nina said, shaking her head. "But what's here isn't working for me. And I don't like that dress at all. The bodice drapes oddly."

Kenzie agreed. Nothing about Nina was average. She needed an amazing gown. She needed a Carolina Herrera dress, or an Oscar de la Renta. She could afford any dress she wanted.

"I love the sleeves on this one," Nina continued, "and I like the drape of this skirt and the neckline on this one. If only I could put all these elements together, then I would have the perfect dress."

"Maybe you should buy all five dresses and let Kenzie remake them," Grace offered.

Kenzie could see the attendant's eyes light up at the commission this sale would give her.

"Let's have lunch and talk it over." Kenzie turned to the saleswoman. "I'm not promising anything, but can you hold these dresses for an hour or two while we talk about it?"

"Of course," the woman said with a warm, practiced smile. "I can hold them until five o'clock."

They walked down the block to a small diner. The diner had a fifties look to it, with red vinyl booths, chrome molding, a white tiled floor and a jukebox in a corner. Each booth had a small, plastic replica of the jukebox listing the songs and a slot for coins to place an order. Currently, Chubby Checker's "Rock Around the Clock" blasted out through the loudspeakers.

"You weren't as much help as I thought you'd be," Nina said to Kenzie.

"Nina," Grace objected.

"She's my best friend, Mom. She's been picking out her own clothes since she was six. She knows fashion better than the two of us put together."

Kenzie grinned. "I have a lot on my mind. And I did offer to have several dresses sent from my contacts in Paris."

"I know, but I'm the bride and it's supposed to be all about me. Besides what bride doesn't want the experience of trying bridal gowns?"

"Two weeks ago, you didn't want to go near a bridal salon. You are so lucky you're my best friend, or I'd bop you on the head." She held up her wrist and pointed at her watch. "You can whine for ten minutes. And then you're going to do it my way."

A waitress placed menus down in front of them and took their drink orders.

"This wedding stuff is complicated," Nina complained. "Maybe we should just elope."

Grace slapped her daughter's arm. "Not on my watch, you don't."

"You put together international marketing campaigns," Kenzie said. "You've worked with people you hated. How can this be complicated?"

"Because I feel like the rest of my life is going to be determined by my wedding day." The waitress brought their drinks. Nina took a long sip of her soda.

"You know it's not," Grace said soothingly.

"In my logical head, yes."

"You and Scott," Kenzie said, "are going to be just as happy if you do a drive-through wedding chapel and get married by Neptune, the sea god."

"Or Elvis," Nina said with a short laugh. "I can just see me now, waltzing down the aisle to the strains of 'Jailhouse Rock.'"

"There's some irony to that." Kenzie stirred her vanilla malt shake and took a sip. She hadn't had a decent shake in years and this was perfect.

"I've made a decision," Nina said. "I'm going to let you order those dresses you wanted me to try on originally. So order away. I am done whining."

"Good. But you still have six minutes left."

Nina frowned at Kenzie. "Have you found your maid-of-honor dress? I know my sister wants to wear something strapless. But I really wanted slip dresses."

Lola, Nina's sister, had deferred all decisions to Kenzie, because she was busy writing the musical score for an upcoming movie and didn't have time to shop. "We decided on midnight blue and found a Monique Lhuillier ballet-length dress that looks good on both of us. Hers is strapless and mine is the slip-dress style you wanted. We're also coordinating with Hunter and Donovan, who will be wearing matching Armani tuxedos."

"Good. That's off my plate and taken care of."

"Hendrix is taking care of the cake and Donovan has the food. The music has been decided," Kenzie said. "By the way, how are the dance lessons going with Scott?"

"It's a good thing I love your brother. He has three left feet, but he is trying." Nina sighed.

The waitress brought their burgers. Kenzie didn't realize how hungry she was until she took her first bite. "This is delicious."

"I agree," Grace said, digging in.

"At least Scott doesn't confuse you," Kenzie said.

"He's still a mystery. That's half the fun. Carl was never mysterious." Nina popped a French fry into her mouth.

Carl, Nina's ex-husband, had always been an open book to Kenzie. The question had always been, why had Nina married him? Knowing the answer would never come, Kenzie thought about Reed. She didn't understand him, either. "I have the same problem with Reed."

"You girls," Grace said. "There's nothing mysterious about love."

"Everything is mysterious about love. I can't interpret Reed's body language. At times, he seems like a gawky nerd and at other times he's so self-assured and confident."

Grace laughed. "Men like a done deal."

"What do you mean?" Kenzie asked curiously.

"Men," Grace continued, "don't mind working for things as long as they have the outcome they want. All of their lives they're taught that if they accomplish all these things, the woman they want will just fall into place like the last piece of a puzzle. And then when the woman is too easy to get, they're bored."

"You mean I have to play hard to get. I don't even know if I want to be gotten." Kenzie stared hard at Grace.

"Sam did a number on her," Nina explained to her mother.

"I never met Sam," Grace said, "but from the first comment Nina made about him, I didn't like him."

"You ran down my boyfriend to your mother," Kenzie cried.

"Oh no," Grace said, patting Kenzie's arm, "Every time she talked about him, her face would get all scrunched up like she'd eaten a bad piece of fish. I don't think she was even aware of it."

"I never said anything bad about Sam," Nina put in. "I just never said anything good."

Kenzie covered her face with her hands. "Why is boyfriend hindsight always twenty-twenty?"

"Because," Grace said, "smart girls learn from their mistakes."

"Being married to Carl," Nina said, "was like being a nanny á la Mary Poppins. I always had to make magical things happen…for him. He really was a good starter husband."

"Looking back at Sam, I can see he needed to feel more important than me. And as impressive as I was, he had to feel superior." She didn't consider the time spent on Sam completely wasted. She'd learned a lot about fashion from him and met a lot of knowledge-able people in the industry.

Grace tilted her head at Kenzie. "What did you like best about him?"

"He loved to shop." Some of the best times she had with Sam were shopping. "And I could take him anywhere and he would never embarrass me. He had beautiful manners, could hold a decent conversation and he was very charming."

"Charming," Grace said with a frown, "is always one of those words that make me nervous when a woman uses it to describe a man."

"What do you mean by that?" Kenzie asked.

She sighed. "Charming is play-acting. Charming is someone who is always on a stage. Charming always seems like nothing more than a means to an end."

"You and Miss E.," Kenzie said, exasperated, "are always throwing out things to think about."

Grace laughed. "That's what old women do. We make younger women think."

"Thanks so much, Grace."

Nina held up her hand. "I don't have to think about things anymore. I have the man. I'm done."

"Oh no, honey," Grace said, "you're in phase one. Phase two is babies, a mortgage, minivans…and phase three…" Her voice trailed off.

"No." Nina's voice was firm. "There will be no minivans in my future."

"Hunter said the same thing," Kenzie laughed. "Five seconds after Lydia said she was pregnant, he was at the car lot looking at minivans. And now they have one." The new baby had triggered something in Kenzie, something she never thought she'd feel.

"No. No." Nina looked horror-struck. "I'm not going to be domesticated."

Kenzie burst out laughing. "But domestication is going to look fabulous on you."

Nina covered her face with her hands and groaned.

"And to get you started on the right foot, I'll call Paris as soon as we get home and place an order for you. Trust me, you'll look fabulous."

A knock on the door to his suite revealed Kenzie standing in the hall with a plate of cupcakes held out in front of her. "I come bearing gifts."

Reed grinned, delighted to see her. His heart started racing and he felt a little tongue-tied. He swallowed the lump in his throat and took a deep breath. "You made me cupcakes?"

"We'll go with that."

He stepped aside and gestured her into the suite. She stepped inside, heading toward the kitchen where she unwrapped the cupcakes and set the plate on the snack bar.

Reed had his laptop set up on the counter. "I've been working on your software."

"How's it going?"

"I haven't revolutionized the fashion industry yet, but I'm making progress." He turned the laptop so she could see the screen. "I've managed to correct most of the errors in the software and simplified it. Instead of putting in a customer's measurements, I've created templates for extra small, small, medium, large and extra-large. I've also done some research on body shapes and I'm including pear-shaped, hourglass, round, etc. I haven't added those modules yet, but I think you'll end up with a satisfying assortment of body shapes for your customers to choose from. My next task is to reconfigure some of the dresses to make sure they will fit properly." He didn't add that this whole process would be time-consuming, but he'd found himself enjoying it. "I've been forced to pay more attention to clothing. Men's clothing is rather simple compared to women's clothing." He opened the wine cooler and pulled out a bottle. He opened it and poured them both a glass.

Kenzie sat on a bar stool and peeled the wrapper away and a took a bite of the cupcake. "Well that's because the average man won't spend the money, and men don't shop the same way women do. My brothers always know what they want, pick it out and leave. They don't browse, they don't wander the aisles, nor do they try things on. They get what they want and get out.

"Hunter either looks like a banker or a construction worker. Scott wants to look as intimidating as possible and according to him, black doesn't show blood. Donovan lived in Paris. When he wasn't in his chef's uniform he dressed pretty snappy, but that's his own personal style."

Reed shrugged. "I'm guilty of throwing on whatever I can find." He couldn't help but admire what she was wearing. "So tell me, is it casual day for you?"

She glanced down at her jeans. "I like red and skinny jeans always look good." She plucked at her T-shirt. "And white goes with everything."

"I heard skinny jeans are bad for your health."

She frowned. "What do you mean?"

"I heard that they can be too tight and can interfere with the reproductive aspect of being a woman."

She grinned provocatively. "I've heard the same things about men wearing tighty-whities."

"That's why I'm a boxer man," he said proudly.

Did that just come out of his mouth? Damn, he was so unsmooth.

Her eyebrows lifted. "Are you thinking about having children?"

He got the strangest sensation that she was picturing him in his boxers and frankly, the thought excited him. He got little tingles down his spine. He liked it. "Someday. What about you?" For a brief flash, he thought about having children with her. They would make beautiful children.

"I'm thinking about thinking about it."

"Why are you thinking about thinking about having children?" This was not the conversation he'd picturing having with her, but he didn't feel as uncomfortable as he thought he would. But then again he really liked her and she made him think about thinking about things. All sorts of things…like the way she would look in his bed with her eyes all sleepy after sex and her body curled around his. He took a step back from her.

"Certain things have to fall into place."

"Such as," he asked curiously.

"Number one, I have to find the right man." She bit into her cupcake again and chewed, a thoughtful look on her face. "Number two, the time has to be right."

"That's a tall order. Nothing ever happens at the right time. You just do it."

"Is that your new philosophy, 'just do it'? I could have sworn you were a planner."

"I had a vision about the near future. I worked my butt off and overcame my fear. Long-term planning is something else. You can't really plan for that. You can have a goal, but things change as you proceed.

You have to remain fluid and change with the challenges." *Listen to me, Mr. Zen Master.*

She studied him. "Funny, I thought you just put your head down and worked hard…with a plan."

"Ninety percent of the world works hard, but not everyone has a plan." He leaned against the snack bar and thought about how delicious she looked, how tempting it was to lean over and run a hand down her arm. He pushed back before he gave in to the temptation. No matter what Miss E. had said, he had to maintain his distance with her. She was seductive and alluring. His fingers itched to touch her, to caress her, to… He had to stop thinking about her.

"What's your next plan?" She traced a pattern on the Formica.

"I plan to seduce you."

She looked startled, then grinned. "I'm the one who brought you cupcakes. Maybe seduction is my plan."

"I planned for you to bring me cupcakes."

She stared at him intently. "Really?"

"It worked. You did." He pointed at the plate. "See? Cupcakes."

Her eyes narrowed. "What are you planning next?"

"My near future plan is to perfect this software and win your undying gratitude." And love. "My current plan is to eat these cupcakes…with you."

Chapter 7

Kenzie sat in her office glancing through the bills on her desk that needed to be sent to accounting for payment. She was elated to notice that the sales of high-end items had increased over 15 percent. Not bad. She made a note to mention it at the next staff meeting. Her salespeople were doing a good job.

Reed walked in after a short knock on the door. "You have a happy look on your face." He held a duffel bag in one hand and was dressed in tan cargo pants, a blue shirt and windbreaker. She wondered where he was off to.

"I do! I'm happy. Sales are improving for not only the regular sales, but the high-end items."

"What does that mean?"

"More swag for me and my sales staff because nothing says success like free stuff." She loved swag.

Nor for herself so much but for her staff. She wanted her people to feel appreciated.

"What kind of free stuff?" He sat on the edge of her desk smiling at her.

His nearness, the faint aroma of spice from his aftershave and the intensity in his blue eyes set her pulse racing. "We...um...we...scored some Michael Kors purses and some...La Perla lingerie." The lingerie had been a bonanza.

"You mean free panties!" He looked confused.

"Lingerie and fragrances," she supplied.

"How do you divvy up the goods?"

"Lottery. Everyone puts their business card in a fishbowl. We draw a card and the first person gets to pick from what's been sent to us. And then the next person can choose, etc."

"Very democratic," he said. "What did you score?"

"Givenchy La Rouge Intense Color Lipstick in Rose Perfecto." She loved the color and the way the lipstick performed. "I traded Fendi sunglasses for the lipstick."

"If you get to choose what you want, why trade?"

"Sometimes you get what you want and sometimes you get what's leftover that someone else decides they want more." She was always willing to trade. "It's a way to bond with my people. You bowled with your people, I share goodies."

Technically she could keep the goodies for herself, but she wasn't that kind of person. She believed in rewarding loyalty and making her people happy. When she'd been a buyer, she had kept a lot of stuff for herself, but she still shared with her assistants. Most of her current salespeople worked at just above minimum wage and they worked hard for her. Sharing the benefits made her feel good and allowed her staff to dress in ways they would never have dreamed. She gave them a clothing allowance and let them buy clothes at cost within reason and taught them how to encourage the customer to buy. *Which was why the software Reed was fixing was so important.* It would be another tool to help the staff show off the beauty of the clothing.

"So what can I help you with?" she asked. "Trying to impress someone?"

"Actually, I'm hoping you'll help me kidnap you," he replied with a wicked grin.

Now that sounded interesting and unplanned. "Kidnap me?"

He glanced at his watch. "You said to do the unexpected. I don't think you woke up this morning thinking you were going to be kidnapped."

She held up a hand. "No, not on my to-do list. Why are you kidnapping me?"

"Why does anybody kidnap someone?"

"To do them bodily harm and get a large ransom."

"I'm a semi-Buddhist and have my own money, so bodily harm and ransom are not in my wheel house."

She frowned at him. "What's a semi-Buddhist?"

"More of a cafeteria Buddhist. I choose what I like and don't bother with what I don't want." He grabbed her hand and pulled her to her feet. "Let's go."

"Go where?"

"I already told you. I'm kidnapping you. Part of the scenario is that you're not supposed to know where I'm taking you while waiting for the ransom."

She stood. "I'm in, as long as it doesn't involve duct tape."

He tapped his forehead with the palm of his hand. "Damn, I'll have to scratch that off my list."

He'd taken her advice to heart, to do the unexpected. And she was intrigued by what he had in mind. He picked up the duffel bag.

"What's in the bag?" she asked.

"Tools of the trade."

"I hope that's not a saw with plastic bags, chloroform or things like that."

"If I told you that, there'd be no surprises."

She studied him and he half pulled her through the boutique to the hotel lobby. "Can you at least give me a hint so I'm not totally surprised?" She glanced down at her cream dress and red wedge shoes.

"It's cool stuff."

She rolled her eyes. "Not much of a hint."

He held up his head. "I'm winging it."

A limousine waited at the front doors. Her grandmother's new chauffeur waited for them. He tipped his visor at her and opened the door.

"My grandmother is part of this, isn't she?" Kenzie asked as she sat down.

"I have no idea what you're talking about." He whipped a scarf out of the pocket of his jacket and started to wrap it around her eyes.

"What are you doing?" She pushed the scarf up to study him.

"No good kidnapping works unless the victim is blindfolded."

She settled back against the cushions. "You are a planner."

"Yes, I am." He put a glass of wine in her hand. "Sit back and relax. Trust me."

"Do you know what it's called when a victim trusts their kidnapper?"

"What?"

"Stockholm Syndrome. Which means when I testify against you in court, I'll have romanticized our relationship."

"I haven't planned your testimony yet."

"You better start now. I'm already thinking about my outfit and the right facial expressions." The limousine slid smoothly into traffic. Kenzie did as Reed told her. She sat back, prepared to be amazed.

The drive was long, but pleasant. Kenzie wanted to ask questions, but knew Reed wouldn't answer them. She'd leaned her head back against the headrest and allowed the drive to lull her into peaceful serenity. Soft music filled the cab of the limo.

The limousine rolled to a stop after what seemed like a much longer trip than Nina thought. The door opened and Reed helped her out. She raised her hand to remove the blindfold, but he stopped her.

"Not yet." He led her down a graveled path that turned into wood. She could hear birds chirping and calling and the sound of waves hitting against sand.

With a flourish, Reed removed the blindfold and Kenzie stood enchanted. In front of her the majesty of Lake Tahoe spread out to reach the Sierra Nevada Mountains. The sparkling clear water shone like diamonds in the sunlight. She stood on a pier with a yacht tied up at the end. Four men in white sailor-type clothing stood at attention on either side of a ramp leading up to the side of the yacht.

"What?" she asked turning to Reed.

"Come on." He grabbed her hand and led her down the length of the pier.

One of the men came forward. "Welcome aboard the Lady Nevada, Miss Russell, Mr. Watson. I'm Captain Nathan Pierce." He introduced the crew.

She didn't think anything could surprise her anymore, but Reed had. "What's going on?"

Reed practically quivered with excitement. "We're going to cruise the lake and Fannette Island. After that, a sunset dinner."

"I'm impressed." She walked up the gangplank to the boat. Reed held her hand as she stepped onto the boat. "I'm hardly dressed for a cruise."

He held up the duffel bag. "All taken care of courtesy of Nina and your grandmother."

"Your co-conspirators. I can't believe Nina was able to keep your secret." Nina had never kept a secret in her life. She wasn't surprised about Miss E. Her grandmother could keep secrets with the best of them.

"Amazing, what the threat of ruining someone's digital life will do." He grinned.

"That would be enough. She's never without her phone or iPad."

The yacht rocked slightly as the crew prepared to cast off from the pier. She followed Reed into the interior of the boat. A dining table had been set in the main salon. He led her to a stateroom and handed her the bag. "Go change. Put the hiking gear on."

"And what are we hiking?"

"We're hiking Fannette Island. It's not too big, but it is rocky according to Captain Pierce."

She took the duffel and closed the door. She unzipped it and pulled out jeans, a T-shirt and hoodie along with hiking boots. As she changed she thought about Miss E. Obviously both Miss E. and Nina liked Reed and they wanted to give him a chance with her.

Sam had wanted to possess her and not in a good way. She had been an accessory for him. Reed was so different. He wanted to make her happy, to be a team, the way Lydia and Hunter were a team along with Nina and Scott and Donovan and Hendrix. She wasn't sure she wanted to be a team yet, but she liked the potential. She smiled as she changed and wondered what was going to happen next.

Fannette Island was the only island in Lake Tahoe. Situated in Emerald Bay, the island was a small, rocky place containing pine trees, shrubs and a building that looked like a tiny castle. The roof on the little structure was long gone and the interior was filled with shrubs, but it had charm. Kenzie perched herself on a boulder to look around. The water surrounding the island was dotted with boats and tourists. She could hear laughter from a group of kids jumping from rock to rock.

Landing on the island had been an experience. It had no beaches, just rocks. The island was so peaceful, she could stay for hours just sitting and gazing at the bay. She turned to study Reed. She liked the way his pants fit him. He wore a dark blue T-shirt and a windbreaker. Even though the day was warm, the light breeze had a cold edge to it, a signal that winter was on its way.

"What is this tiny house that sort of looks like a castle?" Kenzie asked, pointing at the building.

"It was a teahouse," Reed said, consulting the brochure the captain of the yacht had given him. "Built by Lora Josephine Knight. She brought her guests here to have tea. She also built Vikingsholm Castle, which was her summer home." He pointed to a building partially hidden by the trees on the opposite shore. Visitors hiked around the stone house.

"I could have tea here," Kenzie said. She stood on the boulder and looked out over the crystal-clear water of Emerald Bay. "Though it is a hike." Practically straight up.

"Still can't peg you as a nature girl." Reed sat down on the rock next to her and gazed around him. His face and body were relaxed. A boyish look on his face told her he was enjoying himself.

"I like that I can surprise you." Miss E. had always been frugal, with her eyes firmly planted on seeing everyone go to college. Vacations had been camping trips to Yosemite or the Grand Canyon. Kenzie had asked Nina once if she wanted to go camping and the look of horror on Nina's face had been priceless.

A few tourists explored the island with them. Boats anchored offshore contained more tourists, cameras hanging around their necks as they snapped photos.

Reed chuckled. "That's funny. You volunteered for this. I was forced."

"Forced in what way?" Kenzie asked. She studied the shoreline of the bay. Mountains rose in the distance with snow-capped peaks.

"I was perfectly happy being home with my video games and my computer parts, but my dad had this strange notion that fresh air was healthy."

"The horror." Kenzie shaded her eyes. On the far shore a small herd of deer picked their way delicately through the trees. Overhead, an eagle circled lazily, drifting on the air currents.

"I know. Who knew learning to build a fire or a shelter, or finding your way out of the woods would ever come in handy."

"Did it?"

"One time I rented a cabin and took my company to Colorado for a ski bonding weekend."

"Did you enjoy yourself?" She loved to ski. She could hardly wait for the first snowfall at Mammoth so she could break out her snow gear.

"It was cold," he said. "A storm moved in. The electricity went out and we had no internet. Fortunately I knew how to build a fire to keep everyone warm. Or we would have been in trouble. Had we had access to the internet we all would have been fine because we could have searched for how to build a fire, but we didn't. So I built the fire, and set out the game of Monopoly to keep everyone entertained, and I did send a thank-you to my dad for making me learn."

She found herself laughing, imagining him hunched over a fire, coaxing it to burn. That was in conflict with the way he presented himself. "Did you get any skiing in?"

"We got on a plane the day the storm broke and decided our next team-building weekend would be in Cancun."

"There are hurricanes in Mexico."

"My dad taught me hurricane survival, too." His eyes twinkled as he laughed.

Kenzie liked how his blue eyes sparkled when he was making fun of himself and the way his smile appeared when he was talking to her. He was such a handsome man. In the real way, not too fussy, but someone who seemed comfortable with himself. "That's pretty cool."

"I'm covered for hurricanes, tsunamis, avalanches, and the zombie apocalypse."

"The zombie apocalypse, now that's a worry. Having you around for one will be handy."

"I'll save your brain, unless you're one of the people turned into a zombie—then I'll be putting one between your eyes. My dad made sure I could shoot at marksman level."

She loved how he looked so serious. "Scott taught me to shoot." She didn't particularly like guns, but understood why he wanted her to know how to use one. "He'd also taught me how to defend myself, as one of my high school boyfriends found out…the hard way." She could still see the look on Michael Craft's face when she tossed him on his butt. He'd never asked her out again, which was fine with Kenzie. In fact, most of the guys who wanted to ask her out had to think twice about doing so.

"I can do you one better," Reed said with a mischievous grin. "My dad was stationed at the Naval Air Station at Point Mugu just before it became Naval Base Ventura County. I was on the sharp-shooting team in high school. One day, I was walking home from school and decided to practice and accidentally shot out one of the electrical transformers that supplied the base with electricity. I got home from school to find the base on high alert."

"I'll bet your dad had something to say to you."

"Actually, I just cleaned my rifle, put it away and never said anything to anybody."

She gasped. "Love that. And now I have blackmail."

He just grinned at her. "I did eventually confess, but I waited ten years. There was a big contribution to the Wounded Warriors project after that."

She found it difficult to picture him as a teenager. He had such an air of seriousness about him that she felt he'd always been an adult even when he'd been a child. Scott had that same air about him. Meeting Nina had changed him, though. Nina was good for her brother.

Reed stood next to her on the boulder. She could feel the heat radiating off his body. Her heart raced and she was surprised she wasn't all tongue-tied. She pointed out the deer across the water on the other shore and he smiled as he watched them with her.

Reed was a comfortable man to be around. He was amusing company. She could be herself with him. She didn't have to be on her best behavior. For the first time in a long time, she felt relaxed and carefree. She thought about Sam and knew he would never tell her a story about himself that would make him look like a dork. Reed thought his dorkiness was a learning experience. He was an innovator and knew that every accomplishment came with a million failures. That was not only attractive to her, but exciting.

A light breeze caressed his face and ruffled his blond hair and she wanted to run her fingers through it. She suspected he would let her. Below her the yacht bobbed in the water next to another chartered yacht. Captain Pierce stood on the deck talking to a man in the neighboring boat. A couple speedboats roared by, the rippling waves causing all the other boats to bob even more.

"Lake Tahoe has its own Loch Ness monster." Reed held up the brochure. "Called Tahoe Tessie."

"Did you say Taco Tessie?"

"No. Taa-hoe Tessie." He snickered for a second. "Here I was having a vision of a huge taco swimming in the Lake."

Kenzie laughed. "When my grandmother first asked me to come to Reno, I wondered what I was going to do. Living in New York City, you get spoiled with the variety. There's a new restaurant, a new play, a new night club or a new boutique to go to every day. The things to do in the city seemed as if they were designed to distract a person. But here, I have to engage with things. In New York, I felt like a viewer. Here, I can think and enjoy the quiet."

"Some people say peace and quiet is overrated."

She jumped off the boulder and leaned against it. "I used to be one of those people."

He slid down next to her. "What do you think changed you?"

She thought for a moment. "Whether it's 2 a.m. or 2 p.m., Manhattan is never quiet. Here, I can hear myself think." A couple of teenagers approached the old teahouse. Their laughter rang through the stillness. "When I was a kid my brothers and I had to make our own fun even though we lived in Las

Vegas. I feel like I don't take my life for granted here."

"I don't picture you taking anything for granted."

She could feel his steady gaze on her and a heated flush climbed up her cheeks. "I take a lot of things for granted. In an odd way, I took my ex for granted. He would always be there to entertain me and keep me up to date on all the latest gossip, the latest trends." She sighed. "I was shallow."

"What's different now?"

"My family is expanding. My brothers are all in love. I have a nephew and a niece. Every day I see my best friend who is soon to be my sister-in-law. Before, when we got together we would pack so much into so little time. Like we were missing each other because we had things we needed to do. I forgot how much I just enjoy their company, how smart and witty my grandmother is. My world has slowed down to the point where I can actually enjoy it."

"What can I say? I'm semi-retired."

"You work." From what she could see, he worked hard.

"My work is now so much more fun and so much less stressful I feel like I have a hobby I do every day now. My father thought he was going to die after he retired. Instead he fishes, plays golf, romances some really hot babes his own age and works on his old Chevy Malibu. He donates time to a youth program and his church. When he was sick, I got to spend time with him and discover him as a man and a human being. I had no idea how much I liked him."

"I forgot how awesome my brothers are," Kenzie

said, "and how much we like each other. I feel like I have the best of both worlds."

"What do you mean?"

"I get to be independent and yet still dependent on them in a way."

"Until I met your family, I didn't miss having siblings. I wondered what it would be like, but I didn't miss it."

"For the most part it's great until you have a house with only one bathroom. Being the only girl, I always felt I should get the bathroom first."

Reed laughed. "Duly noted. Let's seal the bargain." He leaned toward her and kissed her lightly on the lips.

His breath was sweet and fresh and his lips soft. Kenzie wanted more than just a light kiss. Every inch of her body strained toward him. But laughter from behind them stopped her. She glanced back at the teenagers who watched her and Reed avidly. She blushed.

Reed jumped to his feet, pulled her erect and started down toward the yacht.

From the back of the deck, they watched the sunset. The sun, a brilliant orange, sank behind the mountains. She'd changed out of her hiking clothes into a revealing black dress with a neckline that dipped daintily between her breasts. He'd been pursued by some beautiful women. He'd indulged in them because he was a man, but Kenzie was different.

The waiter poured wine into the glasses while the boat swayed gently as it headed back to the pier.

"Today was wonderful. Thank you for the kidnap

dinner." Kenzie sipped her wine. She shivered and Reed slid a shawl about her shoulders as the night air grew colder.

"Me, too." Never in a million years would he have taken one of the women he used to date hiking and then for a dinner cruise. They would have demanded a refund and called him a cheapskate. Everything that he had done, from dating to mergers, had been to protect the reputation of his company. He dated the kind of women rich men were supposed to date. Kenzie was beautiful, intelligent, witty and stylish and he felt lucky that she was with him. He loved her kindness, her sense of fun and her sassiness. And she took such pleasure in simple things like hiking up a rocky island to look at a broken-down teahouse.

They moved inside to eat dinner.

The waiter served freshly caught rainbow trout with a delicate white wine, asparagus and tiny purple potatoes. Reed watched Kenzie's face. She looked so beautiful in the flicker of the fake candles on the table. He'd wanted real candles but the captain had vetoed that idea.

"Can I have five seconds to talk about business?" Kenzie asked.

"I'm always about the bottom line."

"The Mariposa should do this. Buy a boat, hire a crew, rent Donovan and Hendrix out for special occasions like an anniversary or a honeymoon. What could be more exciting than a five-star chef and pastry chef, an elegant yacht and a sunset? If we found a big enough boat, we could squeeze in a string quartet."

"I think it's a great idea, but let me ask you one

question. Were you thinking about this because you were bored today?"

"No, not at all. This was so romantic and exciting and I want other people to have this feeling and I want the Mariposa to give them that."

"I'm in. We'll talk to Miss E. and see what she says."

Once dinner was over, the yacht slid into its berth. The crew wished them good-night and Reed piled their duffel bag back into the limo.

Kenzie was mostly silent all the way back. Once they stood in front of the door to her suite, she studied him. "Want to come in?"

"Do you want me to?"

"Yes."

Chapter 8

Kenzie stood just inside the entryway. Reed looked a little uncertain. To help him understand what she wanted, she ran her hands up his arms to his face and then pulled him to her for a long, deep kiss.

He slid his arms around her and held her tight.

"Are you sure this is what you want to do?" he asked.

"I've never been more certain in my life about anything."

He kissed her again, his lips soft against hers. He palmed one breast, his thumb circling her nipple until it was so taut, she groaned. Heat threaded through her with little explosive vibrations. She leaned against him hearing the deep thud of his heart and his quick indrawn breath.

"Thank you for today." She pulled away slightly and took his hand, leading him into her bedroom. The housekeeping staff had turned down the bed and left a little truffle for her on the pillow.

She stood next to the bed and he gently reached for the zipper at the back of her black dress and slid it off. Her dress fell forward, down her arms and then to the floor. He stepped back to look at her. She reached behind, unfastened her bra and tossed it on a chair. With her breasts free, he reached out to trace the darkness of her nipples. His breath took on a ragged quality.

Kenzie reached for him and slowly lifted his knit shirt. He shivered when she pushed it over his head. He drew his arms out of the sleeves and she tossed the shirt away.

He unbuckled his belt, then unbuttoned his pants, the zipper a quiet rasp, and pushed his pants down his legs. She admired his body. Lean with broad shoulders tapering into a narrow waist. His pale skin glowed in the light of her bedroom, catching the golden highlights in his blond hair. She smiled as she pushed off her panties and stood in front of him, unashamed of her nudity. He slid his boxers down and his erection bobbed up. He was so ready for her. She touched the head of his penis with one finger, feeling moisture beading beneath her touch.

He pushed her down on the mattress and leaned in front of her, spreading her legs and leaning in to kiss her breasts. His mouth and tongue moved over the hard peaks of her nipples and desire pulsated through her. She moaned.

Reed lifted each foot, removing her shoes. His fingers caressed the arch of her foot, his fingers so gentle hunger exploded inside her.

Reed looked so earnest yet so sexy. She wasn't sure

what to expect of him as a lover, but this coy mix of gentleness and seduction was not it. He was intoxicating. Her body began to shake and her hand sank into his blond hair. She leaned back, enjoying the sensation. She fell back on the mattress aware of nothing but his fingers on her skin, sliding up the insides of her thighs to reach the hidden core of her body.

She trembled as he slid warm fingers inside her and gently stroked the inner walls of her sex. Hunger grew in intensity and she pulled him up to lie next to her.

He reached toward the nightstand for the condom and she heard the scratching sound of foil being torn open. She watched through the haze of her desire as he put the condom on and then stretched out next to her. He drew her into his arms, her body taut against his while his fingers searched out every curve, every erotic spot he could find.

He kissed each breast tenderly, rolling his tongue around each nipple and then drawing back slightly to blow on them. The heat of her skin and the coolness of his breath sent desire rocketing through her.

"You are so beautiful," he said, his tone almost reverent. "I've never known a woman like you…ever."

"Nor I you," she whispered.

He kissed her, his tongue slipping between her lips to caress hers. His fingers slid across her breasts, down her stomach and between her thighs. She gasped as he gently pushed her legs apart and slid in between them, the hardness of his erection tight against her.

A wave of pure ecstasy crashed over her. She arched her back wanting more, wanting him deep inside her. Wanting him to consume her, to take everything he had to offer. She ached with need, writhing against him, the scent of her arousal strong.

"Reed," she half pleaded.

"Yes, Kenzie?"

"Inside me. Please. Now." Her voice was harsh and demanding.

Slowly he entered her, moving deep and steady. Her vagina clenched around him. Passion exploded, and her orgasm began slowly, increasing in intensity until her whole body shuddered.

He pushed deep inside her, each stroke adding to the passion building until she fell over the edge, over and over, her body pulsing with each spasm. She was on fire.

The spicy scent of sex clung to the air. He thrust one last time, his own exploding orgasm intense and strong. He groaned, shuddering with each explosion until he went limp, spent.

He rolled to her side, one finger lazily circling her navel. "That was nice."

She laughed against his mouth. "Nice? Only nice?" This had been earth-shattering to her.

"I think we can do better." He kissed her breast, his tongue lingering on her tight nipple.

"This would probably kill me if it got any...nicer."

"Me, too," he whispered against her ear.

But what a way to go. She snuggled against him and fell asleep to the deepness of his breathing as he fell into sleep against her.

Chapter 9

Reed could barely concentrate. Each time he tried to focus on the code in front of him, his mind skittered off to the image of Kenzie hot and so passionate, and he grew erect with the memory. He couldn't remember ever having such mind-blowing sex in his whole life. He forced the image of her out of his head. He had to get back to work. Daydreaming wasn't going to solve the casino's problems.

He sent Scott a text. Found something.

Be there in five, Scott texted back.

Reed sat back in his chair, his laptop open in front of him. He'd been chugging coffee for four hours and felt wired. He was a little concerned over seeing Kenzie's brother and hoping he didn't have a big sign on his forehead saying, *I slept with your sister.*

He drummed his fingers on his desk. He'd always

been a private person. He'd never dated anyone in his company. He didn't want to be with a woman whose career depended on him. And here he was dating Kenzie, whose whole life overlapped with his. He worked with her, her brothers and her grandmother. Everywhere he turned, Kenzie, or a member of the family, popped up.

He had to find a way to meet with Scott and not give away that he'd seen Kenzie naked. And boy, was she beautiful naked. He'd gloried in the feel of her skin, the softness of her hair and the delicate shape to her breasts. Just thinking about her made him want to hunt her down and take her off for an afternoon of lovemaking.

Scott opened the door to his office and stepped in. "What have you got?"

"I finally found a module that was added to the original programming for the cash cards used in the slot machines." He turned his laptop around to show Scott the lines of code he'd found. They'd been buried deep, but he was good.

"What are you showing me?" Scott perched on the edge of the desk. "In English, please."

"This code here skims five percent off the top of the cash cards when the money is first added. And this line of codes sends the money to a bank account. Here you can see the bank account number and this is the routing number." Reed pointed to the numbers. Scott shook his head. "The routing number is to a bank that I'm pretty sure is in the Cayman Islands." Reed was proud that he'd finally tracked it down.

"Wow," Scott said, frowning. "Can you tell who owns the account?"

"Haven't gotten that far."

"Can you tell how much money is in the account?" Scott asked.

"Not until I hack into it. I just wanted to give you a heads-up that I found this. I found a copy of the original program and set up an app to compare it line for line. Any anomalies that showed I checked by viewing them myself, which is why it's taken so long. It's a lot of lines of code."

"You found it sooner than I expected."

Reed tried not to smirk. "Like you doubted me." The module had been very cleverly hidden and Reed might have ignored it if he hadn't known what he was looking for. "This module was post-added and integrated so carefully that I might have missed it if I didn't know what I was doing."

"A professional programmer had to build this special module," Scott said.

"Yes."

Scott studied the laptop screen for a moment. "I'm glad you're on our side."

Reed was glad, too.

Scott grinned. "Now that's done, how was your date with Kenzie yesterday?"

Reed stared at him, surprised. His stomach knotted up. He had a friend who worked for the government and when he mentioned Scott's name she got this fearful look on her face and told him to be glad he was on his side. "You're her older brother—do you feel comfortable talking about my date with her?" Take the offense, he told himself.

"I'm doing my due diligence as her big brother." His mouth widened into a grin. "And I have video of you going into her suite last night. Late and not coming out until the early morning."

Reed swallowed hard, a dozen images of his death circling his thoughts. "Are you spying on me?"

"I don't spy, I do my job."

"That sounds frightening, overlord," Reed said.

"Did you just use some geek word on me?"

Reed nodded.

"I got it. I'm sort of proud of myself." Scott burst out laughing. "You should see the look on your face."

"Is it fear?" Reed asked. He always thought he was capable of subtle stoicism.

Scott shook his head. "More like defiance. I can respect that."

Reed thought about that. Kenzie was close to her brothers. How much could he admit without getting his fingers broken? Or some organ that was ultimately valuable to procreation. "We had a good time yesterday."

"I'm glad to hear that."

"Are you okay with me dating Kenzie?"

Scott paused. "No."

Was his estate in order, was his will ready? His palms started to sweat. Reed pushed back from the table, too surprised to answer.

Scott burst out laughing. "Of course I'm okay. We're all okay. You're not Sam."

"I could be worse," Reed said.

Scott leaned toward Reed. "Miss E. threatened Hunter, Donovan and me with bodily harm if we mangled you in any way." He cracked his knuckles as though to underscore his comment.

No wonder he had mad love for Miss E. "Thank you."

"Miss E. is the person you want on your side, and she thinks you're all right. She thinks you're good for Kenzie."

Reed didn't realize he'd been holding his breath until his chest started to hurt. He breathed out, relieved. He respected Miss E. "Then I'm going to get back to work. As soon as I have more information for you, I'll text you."

Scott slid off the desk. "Okay. Can you fix it so we can reimplement the software? The casino profits are down. People don't want to deal in money anymore and they want the convenience of the cards and the rewards."

"Easy. It will take me a few hours. I can have everything back to normal by tonight."

"Good. Thanks." Scott let himself out while Reed turned back to his laptop. Reed could have just used the original software and uploaded that to the casino servers, but improvements had been made over the years and he didn't want to lose those improvements. He would just remove the module and fix all the lines of code that pointed back to it.

He set to work, half smiling. This was the part he truly enjoyed.

Lydia sat on the sofa in her family room, the baby in a bassinet next to her. She held a pair of white booties and a white knitted vest, and gushed over them. "Nina, they are beautiful. He will be the best-dressed baby at his christening."

"I know he will." Nina's knitting needles clicked as she worked on a matching hat.

Kenzie constantly marveled at Nina's knitting. Her own gift was a handmade suit in white satin. "Babies in white are so ridiculous. They'll only be clean for a moment and then they'll spit up." She patted little Christian's sleeping face. "You're cute, but you're messy."

"That's his job," Lydia said with a laugh as she unwrapped another gift. Miss E. had a meeting and had simply sent her offering. She opened a box to reveal a silver spoon and matching silver cup with Christian's initials, *CMR*, on the side.

"Up until the time I met Scott, I never wanted one of these," Nina said with a wave of one hand at the baby. "Before Scott, I had Carl and that was baby enough for me."

"How is your ex-husband doing?"

"He discovered he liked the weekly grind of a TV series. He was in the running for a movie, but he turned it down. He likes TV better and the show is doing well in the ratings. The network gave it an early renewal. And his spanking new wife figured out he makes more money doing TV. Also he and Anastasia get to stay in one place." She put down her knitting needles and using air quotes said, "'To solidify their relationship,' as she so informed me. My baby is finally growing up."

"Say what you will about Carl," Kenzie said, "but his ego was always amusing. With Anastasia in the mix, they'll be hilarious for years." She knew Carl had been a handful, but Nina had loved him and in a way still loved him.

"Speaking of exes," Nina said as she resumed knitting, "I heard that Sam has picked his new Kenzie."

"My old assistant is his new project," Kenzie said, not at all surprised at Sam's choice.

"And that was why you and he never worked out. You weren't a project. You didn't need fixing."

"I found that out."

Nina laughed. "You're perfect the way you are and I'm glad you're my best friend." Nina's phone dinged. She pulled it out of her pocket. "Wow, look at that."

"What?" Kenzie leaned over to look at the screen.

"Plane tickets to Florence for our honeymoon," Nina said. "We'll be camping at the honeymoon suite at the de Medici hotel."

"I was there once," Kenzie sighed. The memory of that visit would never leave her. "The butlers have butlers." Sam had rented one and Kenzie had been thoroughly impressed. Though she'd thought they were on a romantic weekend, Sam had been gone longer than he'd been around.

"Scott knows what I like and he's not afraid to pay for it," Nina said with a smug tone. "He'll be getting a little something extra tonight." She winked at Kenzie.

"No, no. Ears burning. Stop." Kenzie covered her ears.

"I heard that a certain computer billionaire, mogul, geek, was seen outside the door to your suite and didn't leave until the wee hours of the morning." Nina grinned at Kenzie. "Spill it."

"Ladies never talk."

Lydia sighed. "So this is what it's like being single, dissecting every romance."

"And doing a play-by-play afterward. You were single," Nina said.

"Saint Agnes is an all-girls' college."

"Doesn't that count?" Kenzie asked.

"Uniforms and no boys."

Nina pursed her lips. "I'm going with no, that doesn't count."

"Had I not ended up with Hunter, I would have wondered if I was missing something." Lydia's smile was wistful and sweet. The baby stirred and Lydia picked him up, patted his diaper and cuddled him in her arms.

Kenzie watched Lydia and the tender way she held her newborn. "I want a baby," Kenzie said and covered her mouth. Had she said that out loud? No, she couldn't have.

Nina burst out laughing. "I know. I want the package, too."

Kenzie said, "So you're going to give up that perfect figure?"

"I'll bounce back, and…" She held her hands out to Lydia. "And for this it would be worth it."

Kenzie understood. She and Nina had been focused on their careers for so long they'd put aside other needs. "How are we going to integrate a career with a husband and family?"

Lydia laughed. "You are both involved in a family business. Stop worrying—there will always be someone to pick up the slack. Miss E. has been waiting for great-grandbabies for a long time. You already have a built-in babysitter. Stop obsessing about it. Hendrix kidnapped Maya yesterday and took her swing dancing. She came home with victory rolls and saddle shoes, singing her off-key rendition of 'Jump, Jive and Wail.' I found her measuring Christian for a baby zoot suit."

"Hendrix is pimping out your baby," Kenzie said.

"So," Lydia continued with a wave of her hand, "the excuse for career versus family is out the window. We're modern women. We'll need to plan our time, but we can do both. Balancing a career and a family isn't going to be easy, but we have each other."

"Miss E. juggled a career with grandchildren and she did it," Kenzie mused. "And she did it with others weighing judgment on her. She was single, black and a woman. Some people told her it was a recipe for disaster."

"You all turned out well," Lydia said, "You didn't even know you were at a disadvantage."

"We got this," Nina said.

"We do, don't we?" Kenzie said in agreement.

Reed had never played dress-up with dolls in his life and here he was doing exactly that. Kenzie, using the camera integrated with the laptop, took a photo of her assistant. Bianca was a short, round woman with pleasant features and blond hair pulled back into a ponytail.

"Do you have enough?" Kenzie asked.

He nodded.

She turned the camera on another of her staff and began taking a photo.

"Is this software going to replace us?" Bianca asked curiously.

"No," Kenzie replied, "it's going to add extra value to you as staff because you can tap into all these different databases and pull out clothes for the customers. But the important part of your job is making the client feel good. Your job is like psychiatry. The hard part is that most of these people you'll never see again."

Both images appeared on the screen. The women clustered around him to watch him manipulate the images. He was especially aware of Kenzie who rested a warm hand on his shoulder. He could smell the faint aroma of her perfume and the heat of her body. Kenzie had become an important part of his life and he wanted to impress her.

"Let's start with Donna Karan."

With a few clicks of the mouse, Reed began pulling clothing templates from the database. He tried to keep it simple so that no matter how computer non-savvy a person was, she could use the program. "Donna Karan's size range is size two to fourteen." He started pulling out a dress and morphing it to both of the models. When he finished they both wore the same dress, but each could see how different it looked on them with their different body shapes and height.

"Wow," Kenzie said, awe in her tone. "That is spectacular."

"I can see all the possibilities," Bianca said. "I can't wait to get started."

"There's more to do. I have a couple bugs yet to track down and repair, and I haven't finished with the final layout," Reed said. "But you'll have this working and ready to use in a couple weeks."

Kenzie hugged him, her scent wafting over him making him even more aware of her closeness. His stomach clenched. "You did good."

"I sort of feel like I'm playing dress-up with dolls." Oops! He didn't mean to say that.

Kenzie laughed. "Hunter and Scott played dolls with me."

"You're kidding, right?" Reed swiveled around to see if she was teasing him.

"Usually when they did something wrong, I black-mailed them into playing with me."

"What about Donovan?"

"When he messed up, he made me cookies."

The other women tittered. Kenzie just grinned at them. Reed wondered how the brothers would feel knowing she was telling secrets out of school.

Bianca raised her hand. "What are you going to give me to keep this secret?"

"Nothing, dear. Tell anyone you want. Spread the word."

"I think I won't," Bianca said with a grin. "I may need blackmail for some other time."

The other women nodded in agreement as they started to back away, breaking into groups. Those still working headed back into the store and those who had just come for the meeting grabbed their possessions and walked out the front door to the lobby.

"Want to go to dinner?"

She glanced at her watch. "I know it's a bit early, but I'm hungry. Dinner is on me."

"I can afford to feed you," Reed objected.

"You have worked your fingers to the bone making me look awesome in the world of fashion. I can afford to buy you a burger as long as you don't want anything worth more than fifteen dollars."

Reed grinned. "Fair enough." He closed the laptop and dropped it into his briefcase. "Where do you want to go?"

"I know a little café with great burgers. It's only a couple miles from here."

"Then let's go." He held an arm out to her. She linked arms with him. Having her so close set his heart pounding into overdrive.

As much as Reed enjoyed eating at the hotel and having the staff fawn over him, he liked getting away. He parked his Lexus in a small lot and Kenzie led him into a quaint café that looked as if it had been opened in the fifties.

"Thank you," Kenzie said. "You made that software incredible and it's going to double the revenue in the boutiques. You are going to copyright it?"

"I already have the paperwork half done."

"Something like this could revolutionize the fashion industry."

He nodded. "It has a lot of practical applications. I already had the core software from the prosthesis application, I just evolved it into fashion and tweaked it." He'd tweaked it a lot, but still, he had to admit in his own sense of pride in making Kenzie look good. He wanted her to look good, to be indispensable to her.

He had enjoyed the challenge. The whole idea of fashion just wasn't on his radar. He knew how he needed to look in the corporate world, but hadn't given thought to how women approached fashion. His company policy had been casual and low-key. In his business people weren't judged on clothes or personality, but on brainpower.

A waitress led them to a table and handed them

menus. He ordered coffee and Kenzie ordered a glass
of water. As they perused the menu, Reed couldn't
stop watching Kenzie. Several men had turned to
look at her, admiration in their eyes and envy when
they gazed at Reed. He felt different around Kenzie,
more alive and happy.

Kenzie had her own glamour despite the designer
dress, tasteful jewelry and fashionable shoes. Her
beauty was incandescent. She glowed with confidence. She was smart and funny. She had a sweetness to her that made him want to protect her. The
women he'd gone out with before had dated him to
have him on their arm. He wanted Kenzie on his arm.
She wasn't an ornament.

The waitress came over and took their order.

"You are looking at me strangely," Kenzie said.

"You are your own practical application."

Her eyebrows rose. "Thank you. I think."

He just smiled at her. "I'm sorry. I'm thinking like
a computer programmer. You are so different from
the types of women I've dated before."

"Are we dating?"

"Yes," he said firmly.

She smiled at him. "Then continue. What about
the women you dated?"

Her smile gave him confidence. It had been a long
time since he'd done this. Dating a woman because
he wanted her. Taking the time to get to know her. He
liked it as much as he'd missed it. She held her glass
with long, slender fingers, her nails polished dark red.
On her thumb and ring fingers, little white flowers
had been painted adding contrast to the brilliance
of the red. Her lipstick matched her fingernails. The

memory of her hands on him sent his senses reeling. He had to remind himself to breathe.

"They had their eye on my bank account more than on me."

"How do you know I'm not doing the same thing?"

Startled, he studied her. He knew she was teasing him, but he hadn't missed that glint of empathy in her eyes. "Because you don't need me. Anything you want, you can get on your own."

"You're not like any man I've dated, either. Though admittedly, my ex-boyfriend was the only one I was kind of serious about."

Knowing what he knew about Sam, he wondered why she dated him. "What about him did you like?"

She tilted her head, pursed her lips, and took a long breath. "In his own way, he was comfortable. He didn't expect anything more from me than I was willing to give and I felt the same way about him. I just didn't know he wasn't what I wanted until Miss E. won the Mariposa and asked me to help her. Then I wanted more and Sam didn't. Sam couldn't imagine himself anywhere but New York. I realized I was tired of New York and wanted to be with my family."

The waitress brought their order. Kenzie had decided on a salad, but Reed wanted The Works hamburger.

"This is good," Reed told Kenzie after his first bite. The burger was juicy, the bread soft enough to soak up the juices, but firm enough not to fall apart. The blend of mayo, mustard, relish and ketchup was perfect. Deep-fried string onions added the perfect tart aftertaste.

"Donovan and Hendrix come here a lot." Kenzie took a bite of her salad. "If you've only dated women who just wanted your money, why *did* you date them?"

"That puts me on the spot, doesn't it?" He licked a finger. Whatever the secret sauce was on the burger, Reed liked it. He wasn't much of a gourmet eater though Donovan was trying to educate him. He just knew what he liked and what he didn't like.

"I'm curious, so answer the question."

He sighed. "Like a lot of men, I'm guilty of taking low-hanging fruit. That sounds pretty bad, doesn't it?"

"What man doesn't want a beautiful woman on his arm? Even my brothers do."

He held up a finger. "But when they started to get serious, they chose women with brains. The fact that they're beautiful is secondary. Your brothers fell in love with what was inside, not outside. Some of the women I dated had brains, but they chose not to use them, preferring to put their beauty forward first. You're an incredibly smart woman who just happens to be beautiful."

She looked a bit uncomfortable over his compliment. "A lot of celebrity women are beautiful, but without makeup they are ordinary-looking. Without makeup, I'm kind of ordinary, too."

He'd seen her without makeup as they shared a cup of coffee the morning after they'd made love. She was stunning even devoid of makeup, captivating in her fresh beauty. "I've seen you without makeup and you're not ordinary. You look young and fresh and pretty in a different way. With your makeup you're polished and sophisticated." He looked her up and down critically. He liked her in both her guises, especially her morning look with her eyes all sleepy and her hair standing up in peaks.

"Thank you, but more importantly you sound like a makeup ad."

"I've been reading those fashion magazines while working on your project."

"And you sound pretty proud of yourself," Kenzie said with a chuckle.

"Those magazines tell you crazy things. Ten articles rhapsodize on the benefits of the ultimate diet, but after reading them, the core of every diet is to eat right."

"I'm sure men's fitness magazines tell you the same thing."

"They're even crazier because they tell a guy to eat right, then have a cheeseburger and a bourbon, but don't forget to work out and get in game time."

"Bourbon, cheeseburgers, video games and a workout. I take it you're not a big fan of men's magazines."

"No, although I did interviews for them. They always portray me as the cool geek, or the hot nerd."

"You don't want to be perceived like that."

"I just want to be a man. I work out because I spend half my life in a chair and it's good for me. High blood pressure runs in my family. I know I don't look like I can bench-press a Buick. Men will never be portrayed as meat, the way women are. There is just as much pressure for us to conform to a certain look as you are."

She ate her salad silently for a few minutes. He could see her turning his comments around in her mind. "That's kind of scathing, considering what industry I'm in."

"If that were true you would never have allowed me to create templates for women up to a size thirty. According to the fashion industry only women sized zero and two should be allowed to be seen in public. But you're making it comfortable for women in larger sizes to buy clothes. I did a lot of research and most of the fancier stores in the other hotels don't carry much of anything over a size ten or twelve. You have beautiful clothes that range from a size two to a size thirty. You want to make sure any woman who shops in one of your boutiques can find something beautiful."

Kenzie nodded. "Trust me, when I wasn't a size two, I felt like nothing. I need to be who I need to be in my size-six body. Look at Hendrix. She's one of the most beautiful women I've ever met and she's a size fourteen and proud of it. Have you seen the way she dresses? When she's not in her uniform, she's a bombshell. Donovan got himself a pin-up girl who can cook. Which totally worked out for him, because men only think about three things."

"We do? What are they and how do you know?"

"Every once in a while there's a good article on relationship psychology."

"What are the three things we think about?"

"Food, status and breeding. Like wolves. In the pack, the alpha is the only one who gets to breed. He gets to be the alpha by eating the most food. Hunter is the perfect example. He got himself a thorough-bred wife because he's awesome and now he has a baby—" she paused for a moment "—and a minivan.

Trust me. I grew up with that man. If he didn't get the last biscuit at every meal, he pouted."

Reed found himself laughing. Everything about Kenzie charmed him, especially her outlook on the world. One woman he'd dated had been so dramatic and jaded he'd been bored with her after an hour. "New York didn't steal your ability to see the wonder in the world."

"After eight years in New York, you'd think I'd be more cynical. For all I know, that's probably why it was so easy to leave."

"I'm glad you did."

"Me, too."

Chapter 10

The conference room had an air of seriousness to it. The walls had recently been painted pearl gray to match the carpet. A solid mahogany table large enough to seat twenty people dominated it. One wall held a huge monitor that normally hid behind sliding panels. A sideboard was laden with a coffee urn, tea kettle, mugs and two dishes of pastries Donovan had brought. Kenzie wanted to add some liveliness to the room with a couple abstract paintings she'd found, but Miss E. said not yet.

Kenzie sat next to Reed at the conference table. He'd called a meeting with everyone, and Miss E. had included Jasper, the previous owner of the hotel, hoping he might know something as well. Jasper, a slim, dapper man in his mid-seventies, sat next to Miss E. His salt-and-pepper hair gave him a distinguished look and the looks he gave to her grandmother made Kenzie think something really serious was going on between them. Every once in a while, Jasper would pat Miss E.'s hand gently.

Hunter sat across from her flanked by Donovan and Scott.

Reed tapped his on his laptop and the monitor on the wall came to life. "This is what I've found so far." He paused as he waited for the screen to catch up with his laptop. "I originally thought the routing number was to a bank in the Caymans, but discovered it's to a bank account in the Seychelles, which is the new financial hot spot for ill-gotten gains now that the Caymans have tightened their regulations regarding money. The account is registered to a company called Preferred Investments." He tapped some more. "I took this investigation as far as I can legally. So I turned what I have over to Scott."

"I don't have the same moral compass," Scott said. "In the event of protecting my family's integrity and reputation, I called a friend in the IRS. They've started an investigation on this Preferred Investments."

"I've heard of this company," Jasper said with a frown. "But I don't remember why I know the name."

Scott nodded. "That's good to know. They may be completely legitimate, or not. Do you remember what context you heard the name?"

"Sadly, no." Jasper shook his head.

Scott continued. "I did find out it's a shell corporation. It has no assets, no information on file except that it's receiving five percent of each cash card purchased in our casino. The money is accumulated over a twenty-four hour period and automatically wired at midnight every day. I have a friend who did a little extra checking and discovered there's only about two thousand dollars in the account at present. And from what he could see the money sits in the account for about two months before it's transferred to another shell corporation registered in Luxemburg and from there it goes to another bank in Hong Kong. We haven't been able to trace anything from there. My friend will keep working on it."

Kenzie wasn't quite certain she understood what her brother was saying, but she did understand someone had been stealing money from the casino. "My question is, if someone is skimming money from the casino, is money being skimmed someplace else?"

Reed grinned at her. "Good question. I checked all the other areas that take in money—the hotel, the restaurants, the bar and shops—and they appear to be fine. The skimming appears to be only in the casino. I plan to check more thoroughly, but the casino is the only place where this scam appears to be in effect."

Miss. E. frowned. "I don't like it when people try to outsmart me. I want whoever is doing this caught and punished. Do we know how much money has been siphoned off?"

"From what I can tell, it's been going on for almost four years," Scott said. "My friend looked through all the past statements for the Seychelles account and a little over seventeen millions dollars has been routed through it."

"That's a lot of money," Jasper said, a serious look in his eyes. "No wonder my profit margin wasn't what I thought it should be the last three or four years. It seemed as though I was losing more and more money and I couldn't explain why."

"Now we know why," Scott replied.

"How do we find out who's behind this?" Hunter asked.

"I'm trying to track down all the officers of all the companies that may have ties to the two major shell companies either directly or indirectly. That's going to take time."

"You said your investigation may not be legal?" Miss E. asked Scott.

"Checking for the officers of a company is a matter of public record, but breaking into the account is something else," Scott said.

Reed nodded in agreement.

Kenzie found herself growing tense. Who would hate Jasper and Miss E. so much that they would try to sabotage the hotel and casino? Considering all the odd things that had happened at the hotel over the past year, she could see someone was trying to make the hotel and casino look bad. There'd been the attempted robbery of the New Year's Eve jackpot money, and then all the kitchen disasters from the fire to the weird tampering with Lydia's cabinet and floor orders. And now the skimming of the cash cards. Were they all related? These annoyances cost time and money because someone had to fix them.

Her phone vibrated. She glanced at the text. It was from Bianca. I have a problem, can you come? "Miss E., I have an issue at the boutique. Can I be excused?"

Miss E. waved her hand. "Of course, we'll catch you up on everything later."

Kenzie smiled at Reed as she stood and stopped herself from bending over to kiss him. That would be bad, especially in front of her brothers. Though she did catch the amused look on Scott's face. Of course he would notice. He noticed everything.

The boutique was in an uproar. Kenzie paused inside the entryway. One of the saleswomen was in a corner dabbing tears away from her eyes. A customer brushed past Kenzie as though in a hurry to get away.

"What is going on?" Kenzie said to Bianca.

"I don't know what to do," Bianca said in a half whisper. "It's Mr. Jasper's daughter and she's just… disrupting everything."

"I'll take over." Kenzie had only met Louisa Biggins a couple of times and had a hard time believing she was Jasper's daughter. They were so different.

Louisa Biggins was a tall, slim woman in her mid-to-late-thirties. She had long, dark brown hair with subtle blond highlights, a narrow face and angry blue eyes. She stood in the large corner dressing room. A pile of clothes had been tossed on the floor and Kenzie tried not to flinch. A Christian Siriano leaf-print sheath lay on top.

"You call this fashion?" Louisa said, whirling around to face Kenzie. She wore an Alexander McQueen kimono of red, white and black that cost three thousand dollars.

"Alexander McQueen does," Kenzie said as she bent to pick up the clothes on the floor, noticing a footprint on a white Donna Karan sheath. She bit her lips at the needless destruction. "If you can't find something in the store, we can order anything you want. We have new software that allows you to try on clothes from a number of designers in a virtual dressing room. It's in the beta stage, but you might find something. Let me take a photo of you and I'll show you how the virtual dressing room works."

Louisa stripped off the kimono and dropped it on the floor. Kenzie caught it before it fell. What she really wanted to do was toss the woman out on her ass, but she was Jasper's daughter.

"Then show me," Louisa said in an imperious tone.

Kenzie grabbed the camera and her laptop and sat down on the chair in the corner, setting her laptop on the tiny round table. She snapped a photo of Louisa and uploaded it into the software the way Reed had shown her. Then she stood and began to show Louisa how to try on dresses.

Louisa sat down wearing her bra and panties. Kenzie grabbed several dresses still on hangers and headed out to turn everything over to Bianca to be re-racked if they could. The Donna Karan would have to be cleaned, but Kenzie would give it to Lydia, who was the same size four as Louisa.

Bianca took the clothes. "We had to put up with her when her father owned the place, but I'd hoped she'd change now that your grandmother is in charge."

"Honey," Kenzie said, "women like her never change." Kenzie had dealt with women just like Louisa before—pampered, bored and brittle. "She's Jasper's daughter, so we'll be as polite as we can."

Bianca just nodded and went to put away the clothes that could be re-racked.

Kenzie returned to Louisa to find her staring at the screen. "This isn't fashion, this is a travesty. Look at this. Size twenty-four. You may as well put this dress on a cow."

Kenzie stiffened with anger. The desire to be polite to Louisa just went out the window. She wasn't about to defend her decisions to this angry woman. "We're done." She snapped the laptop closed and grabbed it away from Louisa. "I don't know who you think you are, but you are not welcome in my store. We don't need your money."

Louisa stood and glared at Kenzie, who glared right back. Louisa huffed. She quickly dressed in a cream-colored sheath, grabbed her purse and opened the door to the dressing room, slapping it against the wall and stalked away.

"I don't like that woman," Kenzie said.

"Nobody does," Bianca replied.

"How did Jasper breed such a harpy when he's so nice?"

Bianca shrugged. "The running bet was that he found her abandoned on the street and took pity on her. Considering the number of husbands she's been through, I don't think they much liked her, either, once her true colors came out."

Kenzie cringed. "What's to like?"

"She used to haunt the jewelry store, make us special-order high-end items and just take what she wanted and leave."

"Did anyone ever complain to Jasper?"

Bianca shook her head. "One time, and after that, we were just supposed to report what she took and Jasper would pay for it."

Kenzie took a deep breath trying to ease the anger that still coursed through her. Maybe she should charge the cleaning bill to Jasper, but shook her head. Jasper didn't deserve to be held responsible for his daughter. No real harm had been done.

"I can clean this," Bianca said. "It won't take much. But there is a little tear in the hem. I can repair that too."

"You can just have the dress, then," Kenzie said. "You earned it. After all, you put up with her for how long before you called me?"

"Too long." Bianca gave a small chuckle. "And thank you."

Kenzie smiled as Bianca took the damaged dress into the back room. The loss of the dress was a small price to pay to keep her staff happy and never have to see that woman in her boutique again.

The door to Reed's office opened and Kenzie peered around the edge. "I thought you were going to San Francisco today."

"No, I canceled." He had too much work to do to head to a comic book convention.

"Canceled what?" She stepped into his office and sat down across from him.

"WC Combo Con." At the confused look on her face, he added, "West Coast Comic Book Convention."

"That sounds like fun. Do you dress up as a super-hero?"

"Not anymore. When I was in high school, I liked to dress up as the Flash."

"The intellectual nerd superhero." She grinned at his embarrassment.

He'd loved dressing up, but the image didn't work

as the executive of a major company and he'd stopped. "Cosplay is a big part of the conventions."

"Cosplay?"

"Costume playacting. Get in character and stay that way through the whole convention." He'd had a group of other high school friends who'd banded together at the conferences. They'd been the object of a lot of teasing in high school. Dressing up as his favorite character had been fun. And he'd been amused when a couple of the bullies from high school had applied for positions in his company. For all their disdain for his choice of entertainment, they'd ended up working for him. He'd personally conducted those interviews and taken great pleasure from the looks on their faces when they'd discovered he was the owner.

"You need to go."

"I just have too much work."

"Take it with you if you have to, but you're going. I'm going with you and I'll make sure you balance work and fun. So get packed, I'll meet you at the front desk in an hour. It's my turn to kidnap you."

She was kidnapping him. Obviously, turnabout was fair play.

He'd never shared this part of himself with a woman he'd dated. And this was his chance to introduce her to his friends. He headed to his suite to pack.

"Ready?" Kenzie asked when he exited the elevator.

He held a backpack with his laptop and tablet in it and carried an overnight bag. "I'm ready."

The drive to San Francisco was pleasant. Kenzie had insisted she drive so he could do some last-minute work. He'd been making sure that various departments at the Mariposa were not victims of skimming, too. So far, as he'd mentioned at the meeting, he'd been able to determine the casino was the only element affected, but he wanted to double-check just to make sure.

She tuned the Sirius radio to classical music and left him to finish his work.

The convention, being held at the Concourse Exhibition Center, was just a few blocks from Mission Bay. When they finally entered the city, Reed pulled up a map and directions on his laptop and directed Kenzie to the hotel.

He checked in while Kenzie parked the car in the small parking structure behind the hotel. He called her and gave her the room number. Just as he was inserting the key card into the scanner, she appeared, pulling her suitcase. Suddenly, sharing a bedroom with her for three nights seemed more intimate than he'd expected.

"What a pretty suite," she said as she wheeled her suitcase into the bedroom.

"I like to be comfortable."

She returned to the living area and went into the kitchenette to open the refrigerator, removing two bottles of water. She handed one to him and sat down crossing her legs while she twisted the bottle open.

"So what's the agenda?"

"First of all, I want to call my friends and let them know I did make it. Then I have to check in at the convention center. Fortunately, I always order a few extra tickets and I will call registration to give them your name. Then we can head over to the convention center and pick up our badges. Tonight is the welcome party and tomorrow the workshops and lectures will start." He handed her a brochure with the list of events.

She opened it and perused it. "I don't even know where to start. I was hoping for drinking and debauchery."

Reed grinned. "That comes later. But right now how about dinner?"

"Where?"

"The Franciscan Crab. It's right on the bay. My friends and I have a reservation for seven thirty."

"Can you see Alcatraz?"

He nodded. "It's lit up at night and pretty spectacular."

"I'm going to unpack. I'm assuming casual is the dress code for dinner."

He nodded. Nothing about Kenzie was casual. For some reason he was anxious to show her off to his friends.

The Franciscan Crab restaurant was an institution in San Francisco, boasting the best crab in the world. Kenzie was impressed as Reed opened the door for her. They checked in for the reservations and were taken up a flight of stairs to the dining area. A bank of windows overlooked the bay and she paused to stare.

Ferries, with running lights, pulled away from the piers. She wondered if they were heading to Alcatraz or just taking people home. A searchlight rotated on the island. A few seals bounced in the water along the pier's edge. A couple of late-night tourists had their cameras out trying to take photos. The flash of the cameras bounced off the water.

She'd been to San Francisco a few times, but never seemed to have time to sightsee. Maybe this time she would.

They approached a long table with seating for six. Three men and a woman immediately stood.

"Kenzie, these are my friends," Reed said. "That's Bob Whittier. He's a graphic artist."

Bob nodded at Kenzie. He looked to be around thirty, with pale blond hair framing a thin face. He wore thick glasses over amber-colored eyes. He gave her a shy smile.

"Tara Preston works for the government in a capacity we can't talk about."

"I'd have to inform my superiors and they'll send out a Special Forces team to take you out." Tara was a tiny woman, maybe five foot two with long, wavy brown hair, hazel eyes and a sweet face.

"This is Seth Powers. He's a wildlife photographer for *National Geographic*." Seth was a sturdy-looking man with graying hair. He gave her a broad smile showing perfectly straight white teeth.

"And finally, this is Arthur Sentovich. He's an engineering professor at MIT."

Kenzie waved at him. She felt a little intimidated by the brain trust. She was having a hard time reconciling these people with their love of comic books and costumes.

Reed seated her at the table across from Tara, who smiled at her. At least she wasn't the only woman.

"And you all know each other how?" Kenzie queried.

"High school," Tara offered with a grin. "We were known as the Geek Squad."

"I hated high school," Kenzie said.

"You? Princess, cheerleader, or prom queen?" Tara asked curiously. She leaned her elbows on the table.

"None of the above," Kenzie replied. High school had been horrible. She had always felt as if she didn't fit in, especially when she wanted to take sewing classes. All the girls had teased her about her habit of wearing the clothes she'd designed herself. In her mind, she'd been more fashionable than all of them put together.

"You're kidding me?" Tara gazed at her, disbelief in her eyes.

"Nope. Decent grades, president of Art Club. But for the most part I kept my head down and tried to stay out of trouble. Vegas is a rough town." Kenzie glanced at the menu. She already knew what she wanted. "You guys know. Independence is not admired in high school. If a girl didn't belong to a particular clique or dated the right guy, they were either ignored or bullied. Let's face it, with my three older brothers—my big, big older brothers—I was not on a lot of guys' social calendars. Which was fine with me. Now, in college, I found my stride. But then again, I had the coolest best friend ever. You don't need to know about me. I want to know about Reed." She elbowed him in the arm. He gave her an uncomfortable look.

"He was the leader of our pack," Bob put in.

"What kind of crazy stuff did you guys get into?"

Reed cleared his throat. "You don't need to know that."

"Of course I do." Kenzie just grinned at him, amused at his discomfort.

He mumbled something just as the waitress came to take their drink order, putting their conversation on hold for a few minutes. Kenzie decided to just have water. She had the feeling she'd need to keep her wits about her with this group of people.

After the waitress left, Bob gave a mild shrug. "Reed and I broke into the locker room and put itching powder on all the jocks' underwear."

"Nasty," Kenzie said in admiration.

"Not really. The jocks picked on us all the time. We were just evening the playing field."

"And," Seth put in, "The jocks stole the biology exam one semester. We stole it back and changed the answers. Boy, that was one epic jock fail."

"Did you look at the answers?"

"No," Seth said. "We weren't going to fail biology. I could have taken the test half-asleep and gotten an A."

Reed nodded in agreement. "High school was boring. It was something to endure before getting on with the rest of our lives."

"I went back home to settle my mom's estate couple months ago," Arthur said, "and I ran into Johnny Morrison." He glanced at Kenzie. "He was the star quarterback on the varsity squad and he has a son who is the biggest geek-in-training I've ever seen in my life. He must have gotten his brains from his mother. Johnny manages an office supply store. His big shoulders have slumped to his middle. He asked me out for a beer, wanting to know what to do about his son."

"Did you laugh at him?" Tara asked.

"No. I just told him to be patient and encourage

him. Be a part of his life and try to get the best out of him."

"My dad was like that," Reed added. "He knew how to get the best out of people."

Tara burst into a laugh. "Yeah, I remember when we tee-peed your house and your dad made us paint the front porch as punishment. I still remember the scraping and sanding we had to do before we could even get to the painting part. And then he spent the next day critiquing our painting job."

Reed joined in the laughter. "That's because my dad hates to paint. And you got off lucky."

"That's because no one ever figured out you're the one who shot out the electrical transformer and put the whole base on alert," Seth said with a grin.

"How did you know?"

"You mumble in your sleep."

"That would be great blackmail material if I hadn't come clean with my dad."

"The statute of limitations is over on that," Tara said.

"Are you all navy brats?" Kenzie asked curiously.

"We are not brats, but navy juniors," Reed corrected. "And, yes. The military is a pretty small place and no matter what base my dad was at, I always knew someone from a previous assignment."

"High school was the only time we were all together at the same time," Tara said.

Their conversation paused as the waitress returned with their drinks and to take their order. Kenzie ordered crab Alfredo and Reed decided on Dungeness crab.

"I'm surprised you all didn't follow in your parents' footsteps," Kenzie said, picking up the conversation again after the waitress left.

"Arthur went to Annapolis," Reed said.

"I'm in the reserves now," Arthur added. "I was the weapons officer on a submarine for seven years. I like submarines, but military life is hard on a marriage. I met my wife in Hawaii and decided I couldn't be away for six months out of every year, so I left active duty for the reserves."

"Where's your wife?"

Arthur grinned. "She's doing a spa weekend with our daughter."

Kenzie could understand the limited appeal of a comic book convention. "Do you all still dress up?"

"Not anymore," Seth said. "We just like to check out the new comics and get together. Maybe do some gaming."

Kenzie gazed at Reed. He was so different, so relaxed. She liked seeing him with his guard down. He glanced at her and she smiled.

Back at the hotel after dinner, Kenzie watched the last person exit the elevator before they were transported to their floor. Reed turned to her and planted his mouth on hers. His hand slipped around her hip and he palmed her butt. Normally this would embarrass her, but there was something safe about being with Reed.

His mouth was so warm and demanding her head was spinning. She felt his hand slip under her dress and caress her bare thigh. If he pushed the issue she'd let him make love to her in the elevator. By the time they arrived at their floor, Kenzie was really turned on. She noticed his hands shook as he used the card key to unlock the door.

Her thoughts were cut off when Reed pulled her over to the dining table in the front room of the suite. The curtains to the balcony were open. Kenzie pushed the doors open and looked out at the night. San Francisco was ablaze with hundreds of thousands twinkling lights. Car lights moved steadily down the streets below.

Reed turned off all the lights and pulled her back into the living room. He took off his jacket and grabbed her tightly.

"What are you doing?" she asked curiously, excitement sizzling through her veins.

"I'm not going to make it to the bedroom." He pulled her dress up and over her head, unhooked her bra and shoved her panties down far enough to insert his fingers inside her.

Desire blossomed and she half groaned. "The bedroom's ten feet away."

He yanked off his shirt, unbuckled his belt and shrugged out of his pants and briefs.

"I'm too turned on. Watching you with my friends tonight was enough to get me started early."

She touched his erection, sliding her fingers down the smooth skin, then up and down again, rubbing the tender tip. "Really?"

"You liked them."

"They made me laugh. You make me laugh."

He buried his head against her neck. "Tonight I'm going to make you scream."

She hoped so.

His fingers slid in and out. He bent her back over the dining room table, spread her legs and pushed himself inside her. Her legs encircled his hips and she realized she still had on her Jimmy Choo stilettos. He ran a hand down her leg and along the peak of her arch.

Kenzie tilted back her head. "Make me scream." She inclined her head toward the open window. "And anyone else who can see in here."

He leaned over and kissed her. "No one can see us except the seagulls."

The idea of an audience of seagulls perched on the balcony railing made her giggle. He thrust harder into her and she gasped.

"Just focus on me. We are the only people in the world."

She could handle that.

His lips were warm and firm and his tongue slipped into her mouth. Reed's hands caressed her bare thighs, massaging her skin until the heat rose and her flesh was scalding. Wetness and heat surrounded her and her nipples pebbled.

Reed ground himself against her. "You make me lose my head."

She couldn't even begin to explain what he did to her. He excited her, made her feel safe and he saw the real her. "Good." She ran her hands up his muscled stomach. His skin was smooth and warm. She loved the way his muscles contracted under touch. The way his nipples got hard under her fingertips. Being with him was intoxicating and she loved that he responded to everything she did. She loved that he seemed to know how she liked to be touched and that she pleased him.

He laughed against her mouth. "Comfortable?"

Surprisingly she was despite the hardness of the

dining table. She didn't know she had this devil-may-care attitude in bed. Sam was pretty conventional. They never would have made love anywhere but in bed and in the good old missionary position.

"Just make love to me. Make me scream, Reed." She reached down and massaged the tender skin of his groin. He reached between them to massage the nub of her excitement.

"Kenzie?" he whispered.

"Now," she said.

He thrust so deeply into her she slid back on the slick table. The heat overwhelmed her and she shifted her hips to take him all the way inside of her. Oh dear God, he felt so good inside her, so powerful. She felt so full, so complete. She braced herself on the table and arched her back to get him all the way inside her. She locked her legs around his waist. He gave her hard, deep thrusts.

How she loved this man. She'd never get enough of him. Her excitement grew as he deepened his thrusts and they grew more savage. Her excitement was almost at the breaking point. Her head fell back and he buried his head in her neck.

"You feel so good," he whispered, his tongue flicking at her lips.

"Harder, please. Harder." Her voice came out in a harsh whisper. "Harder."

Reed grabbed her ankles, pushed her knees up and spread her legs wider. He pounded into her. She felt suspended over a precipice. Her vagina clenched around him and she felt his body tense and a second later she felt him come. He bit down on her shoulder. The pain added to the intensity of her orgasm. Her whole body seemed to explode, each spasm more intense than the last. She shuddered, she scratched his back and finally she screamed.

Chapter 11

Kenzie slanted a look at Reed. She felt warm heat color her cheeks. Last night had been so intense she still felt the resonating orgasms that had consumed her. Not until they'd finally sought their bed, curled in each other's arms, did she remember he hadn't used a condom. She hadn't been on the pill since leaving Sam. Not that she'd planned to be off it, but felt the need to have her body return to its normal rhythm.

They wandered the conference floor. She was completely dazzled by the crowds, the attendees in costumes and even small children running around dressed as Jawas from *Star Wars*. Some of the women were dressed in what Reed told her was steampunk.

"Steampunk?" She stared at a woman who appeared to have a metal corset over a bright tartan skirt that skimmed the floor.

"Have you ever read Jules Verne or H. G. Wells?"

"*Twenty Thousand Leagues Under the Sea.* Yeah. In high school." Kenzie eyed a table laden with banker boxes filled with comic books, all in transparent protective plastic sleeves. She wanted to stop and pick through them, but Reed had already moved on.

"It's now defined as steampunk literature. A number of modern-day authors have continued the tradition and spawned a whole subgenre in science fiction and fantasy literature."

"I'm going to have to read some. Stop. There's a book dealer."

She dragged him by the hand into a booth, marveling at how much she was enjoying herself. Reed directed her to the steampunk section while he browsed the comic book section. She found her attention wandering to a teenage girl dressed in a tight-fitting leather jacket, long green skirt and top hat with goggles on her head. A swirl of her skirt showed Kenzie that she wore laced up boots with kitten heels.

"Can I take a photo of you?" Kenzie asked.

"Sure." She stood straight and posed. Kenzie took out her phone to capture this.

She chose a couple of graphic novels and a book on the history of steampunk, paid for them and went to find Reed.

"I'm so glad we're here, exposing me to the weird and wonderful."

He grinned. "Thank you for saying that with admiration and respect."

She felt sort of silly and carefree. She took his hand and they continued to wander down the long aisles.

"I would never have known about this subculture

if you hadn't decided to bring me." She eyed a woman dressed as a steampunk pirate complete with an eye patch and plastic sword.

"It is fun, isn't it?"

If she'd been in New York, she might have thought all these people were crazy. And Sam would have looked down his nose with scorn at them.

Maybe she needed to indulge, too.

By the end of the first day, Kenzie was exhausted, but she found a pirate costume she had to have. It had a brown leather bustier which laced down the front. The skirt was short, barely covering the tops of her thighs, and a rich brownish gray. She refused to let Reed see it, because she had a use for it later, when they were alone. Yes, they were going to have their own steampunk fantasy.

When they got to the bedroom, Kenzie pointed to the bed. "Make yourself comfortable. I'll be right back." She winked at him.

As soon as the door was closed, Reed quickly shucked his clothes, throwing them on a chair. Then he fell back on the bed and got himself comfortable. He was already erect. Kenzie had a way of doing that to him. He slid his hands behind his head and waited. A few minutes later he saw the light go out under the bathroom door. Kenzie opened the door and sauntered into the bedroom, dressed like a naughty pirate wench. She turned around slowly, the skirt flaring to show she wore no undies. The breasts were pushed so high under the bustier he could see the tips of her nipples. His mouth dropped opened and he couldn't speak. His mouth went dry and the blood raced from his head.

Kenzie perched one hand on her hip and posed. "You like?"

He could only nod. He started to get up, but she pushed him back onto the bed. "I have this."

"Are you my pirate treasure?"

She arched an eyebrow. "You don't have to steal me."

He went twitchy and hot as she pranced around the room before standing next to the bed, flipping up her skirt and sliding over him.

"Tonight it's my turn." She straddled his hips and caressed his chest, his nipples and ran her fingers up his neck to his chin. He caught one finger in his mouth and sucked on it.

A lusty smile, somewhere between seductress and innocent, showed the tiny dimple in one cheek. "Do you want me?"

"Aye, Captain. Very much." His mouth was dry and he wet his lips.

She leaned down and starting at his navel licked her way up his body to his nipples. She rolled each nipple around her tongue and back down to his navel. She slid down his stomach until her tongue reached the tip of his penis. She licked the tip and his muscles tightened, he was so ready to let go right then.

He reached for her. She batted his hands away. "No touching."

"Kenzie," he groaned.

She cupped his balls and began long, strong licks from bottom to tip. Each movement of her tongue brought him closer to orgasm.

"I love touching you," she said.

He could barely breathe, much less talk. He gasped again as her tongue swept across the tip of his penis.

She sat up, eased herself over his erection and lowered herself.

She pushed down hard and started to unlace the bustier. Her breasts fell out and she cupped them, holding out the nipples to him. He reached for her, but she shoved his hands away. "No touching."

She massaged her breasts while he watched, the heat and excitement almost too much to bear. Then she reached down between her fold and began to massage herself. With her eyes half-closed and her lips slightly parted, she looked every inch the wanton.

She leaned forward to kiss him. Her tempo increased. He grew harder and harder. His muscles began to contract and release built inside him.

"You feel so good," he cried.

"Yes," she sighed as she moved over him, her softness giving way to his hardness. The rightness of this was perfect. Reed moved inside her slowly. He never took his eyes from hers. Her hands moved over her slowly and Reed relished every touch, every caress. His jaw hardened as if he tried holding back.

"Love me harder."

"I want it to last," she said.

"We have the rest of our lives." He tensed his hips and thrust hard into her. She clamped her knees tightly about his hips. The tightness in his stomach built and burned. He pushed into her harder and harder until he felt her fly over the edge and a second or two later he came with her.

Chapter 12

Kenzie stood in Lydia's living room. A rack of wedding gowns was behind the sofa and a large mirror leaned against one wall. Lydia had pushed all the furniture out the way so Nina could try on each wedding gown and parade around the room to show it off to Miss E., Nina's mother, Grace, Lydia, Hendrix and Maya. Kenzie made a few minor adjustments to the gown and turned Nina to the mirror.

The gowns had come yesterday and Lydia insisted they have a champagne brunch while Nina tried them all on.

Nina gasped in surprise as she stood in front of the mirror and studied herself. The Marchesa wedding gown was a creamy eggshell white with an off-the-shoulder lace bodice. The skirt was two layers, lace and then an overlay of silk, which cut away to show the heavily embroidered lace insert. The train flowed out behind her for several feet. The style had a vintage, timeless feel to it that gave Nina an elegance that added to her beauty.

"I love this one," Nina said. "It's perfect." She pulled her hair up and wound it around into a knot to show off her long neck.

Miss E.'s eyes narrowed critically. "This dress reminds me of the one I wore when I married your grandfather." Her tone was wistful with the depth of her memories. Her husband had left her before her son was a year old and had never been seen or heard from again. Kenzie often wondered what happened to him.

"I didn't think you'd choose this one," Kenzie said as she stood back and studied the cut of the gown and the way it lay so smoothly over Nina's curves. "Marchesa isn't quite your style."

"It's a little old-fashioned," Grace said and she studied her daughter.

"I know," Nina said. "That's the appeal. I thought I would like something smooth and sleek and sophisticated. But the moment I put this one on, I felt so different. I thought I heard angelic trumpets."

Kenzie circled Nina, adjusting the waist, which was a smidge too loose. She could easily adjust the fit with a tiny tuck here and there and no one would ever notice. "Angelic trumpets?"

"I know exactly what you mean." Lydia clapped her hands. "When I married Mitchel, my mother picked out my gown and I hated it. It was beautiful and elegant with lots of lace and a veil that was ten feet long, but it wasn't me. When I put on my gown to marry Hunter I heard a whole chorus of angels. That's how I knew it was the right one." She glanced fondly at the wedding photo of her and Hunter on the side table. She'd chosen a simple gown with tiny puffed sleeves and a drape of formfitting silk that made her look elegant and perfect.

"I just threw that one in as a ringer to give you a wider selection. I didn't really think you would choose it, because it's more my style than yours." Kenzie glanced back at the rack of gowns in the middle of Lydia's living room. She'd chosen each one thinking Nina would have a hard time choosing. But she'd gravitated immediately to the Marchesa.

"That's why I love you." Nina twirled slowly, watching the flow of the gown in the mirror. "You're my best friend. You know what I need, even when I don't know what I need."

"Keep that thought," Kenzie said with a chuckle. She adjusted the shoulders, pushing the lace down to expose more of Nina's shoulders.

Hendrix nudged Kenzie. "Thanks. How am I supposed to top this?"

"Don't worry," Kenzie said, "Jean Paul Gaultier owes me a favor. He loves rockabilly and that man can design for the juicy girl like nobody's business."

Hendrix grinned. "Today you're my favorite."

"I know." Kenzie bent over to fluff the train out a bit.

"You're so pretty," gushed Maya to Nina.

"Thank you," Nina said, stooping to kiss Maya.

Kenzie helped Nina out of the dress and carefully draped it over a chair. Miss E., Hendrix, Maya and Grace drifted into the dining room where Lydia had set up the champagne brunch.

"What's going on with you?" Nina said as she

stepped into her jeans and pulled a bright red T-shirt over her head.

Kenzie replied. "We can talk later. This is your day."

"We'll talk now. You've been scattered and unfocused since you returned from San Francisco with Reed." Nina stroked the gown, her eyes alight with pleasure.

"I'm fine. Sort of."

"Define *sort of*," Nina pressed.

"Reed and I were just supposed to have some fun. I bought a pirate wench outfit for him and seduced him wearing it. I never bought anything like that for Sam." Sam would have been horrified if she'd tried to seduce him wearing a cheap pirate costume.

Sex with Reed was fun. She almost blushed at the memory of his face when she'd walked out of the bathroom dressed in her costume. Sam never lusted for her. Their relationship had been more of a business merger than one built out of love. She couldn't help wondering why she'd invested so much time in him.

"Yeah, you and Sam were so perfect you were boring."

"What do you mean?"

"Boring is boring. He was tab A in slot B. That works, but there's no excitement. If the world ran on logic, Scott and I wouldn't be together. Honestly, can you imagine me with some anal-retentive, left-brain dominant, uptight, macho…"

"Are you sure you love my brother?"

"I love all those things about him. We're fire and water and make one hell of a soup. You and Reed complement each other. You bring a liveliness to his geekiness. And he grounds you."

"When did you get so smart about men?"

"I've always been smart about men."

"Carl. Remember Carl and your divorce?"

"Carl was a project," Nina said. "Granted I thought he would be a lifetime project, but I miscalculated and that just made me a better, stronger woman who is perfect for your brother."

Kenzie stared at her best friend, remembering some of the guys Nina had dated in college. She'd been in fix-it mode then, too. But when they broke up, the guys were always better. And she always managed to remain friends with them. Even Carl was still a good friend of Nina's. But Sam hated Kenzie. At least she thought he hated her. She'd sent him several texts asking how he was and he hadn't answered.

"I don't know what I'm going to do," Kenzie finally said. "Reed confuses me."

"When you figure it out, then do something. Right now, have fun. But don't cut your nose off to spite your face."

Kenzie wheeled the rack of discarded wedding gowns into the storeroom in the boutique; the casino purchased them outright and would sell them in the bridal salon Kenzie was starting. Miss E. wanted to convert the old amphitheater into a wedding chapel and a wedding boutique for potential brides. Kenzie knew that the certain type of bride who would want to get married at the Mariposa would want designer gowns that cost thousands of dollars. But then again, weddings were big business in Reno.

She flung a sheet over the rack even though each gown was draped in a plastic covering.

"Kenzie," Bianca called out as she walked into the salesroom. "What gown did Miss Nina choose?"

"The Marchesa," Kenzie said still surprised by Nina's choice.

"I didn't see that one coming," Bianca said. "You had a visitor while you were gone."

Kenzie straightened a display of Hermès scarves, refolding a couple and redraping one around the half mannequin in the center of the display sporting a Dana Buchman sweater.

"Who?"

"He didn't say. I told him you'd be back around two."

A customer entered the boutique and Bianca approached the woman ready to offer her services. Kenzie headed back to the cash-wrap counter to finish folding some sweaters. She was deep in thought about the spring line and making notes to herself when she sensed a presence.

Sam Bell stood in front of her. She blinked. "Sam?"

"Kenzie." He leaned over to kiss her, but she backed away.

"What are you doing here? Why are you here?"

Sam was a tall, slim man with an impeccable eye for men's fashion. His gray Gucci suit, with a teal shirt and tie, perfectly complimented his lean physique. His suit didn't cost less than six thousand dollars. And he knew how good it made him look. His black hair was cut close to his skull and a tiny mustache decorated his upper lip. He was a handsome man and he knew it.

"You're so amusing," he said with a forced laugh. "I know how to use Google Earth."

She wondered why he'd shown up in Reno with no

warning. "What can I help you with?" Sam didn't do anything without a reason.

"We're old friends," he said. "Don't I get a hug, at least?"

"No." She wasn't at all pleased to see him. She'd finally managed to get over her disappointment and here he was again.

"I thought you'd be pleased."

Her eyes narrowed. "Why?"

"Let's get some coffee. I saw a cute little café around the corner from here."

She caught Bianca's gaze. "Ten minutes. I'll be back in ten minutes."

She headed out of the store with Sam at her side. "You left your snow globe at my apartment. I thought I'd bring it to you."

"You came three thousand miles to deliver a snow globe that you hate." She studied him, wondering what had really brought him.

"Consider it a peace offering."

They entered the café and found a booth. "I didn't know we were at war."

She sat down. The waitress hurried over and she ordered tea and Sam ordered coffee.

"Those pastries over there look edible. Should I get one?"

The way he spoke about the pastries set her back up. Hendrix was a genius and Kenzie loved everything she made. "You only eat organic food and I can guarantee you there's nothing organic in that case. But if you want something I think the gluten-free muffins should work for you."

"Then I'll have one."

When the waitress brought their drinks, Sam ordered a muffin and Kenzie ordered a brownie.

"Aren't you worried about your weight?" Sam asked pointedly.

"Nope." She refused to be intimidated. "You don't know what you're missing."

"The extra weight does look good on you." He waved his hand as though giving her permission to eat her brownie.

"Thanks," she said. She hadn't gained an ounce since she'd left New York. "Again, why are you here?" She cupped her chin in the palm of her hand waiting for him to get to the reason for his appearance.

"I took a tour of the casino and all the shops. I have to say I'm impressed with what you've done. Who knew a little backwater community like this would attract so many people with money to spend."

Irritation grew. She clamped down on her tongue to keep from snarling at him. How dare he insult Reno? Some days New York smelled like a sewer. Reno never smelled bad. New York was crowded and noisy. Reno was spread out and spacious. She never felt as if she didn't have room to think.

"The men's store is amazing," Sam continued. "I almost bought that beautiful Burberry suit in the window."

"I kept all of my contacts from Saks. Why are you so surprised?"

"Speaking of which…"

"And here's the real reason you're here." She tried to wait patiently for him to get to the meat of the conversation, but Sam was not to be rushed.

He frowned slightly at her. "I know we parted badly."

That was the understatement of the year. His angry voice still filled her mind. His complaints made her furious all over again. And telling her she was selfish had been the final insult.

He took her hand and held it. "You need to come back to New York. We need you. The store needs you. Our clients need you."

Not want me back. But need me back. "What's going on?"

"There's anarchy in the buying department."

"Go on," she said, pulling her hand away. Something about his touch made her uneasy.

"We had to fire Anna."

"The person you hired to replace me? Why? What happened?"

"I couldn't work with her."

"You championed her, campaigning to have her hired."

"She didn't work out. She's not you."

"Nobody is." She smiled sweetly at him. Had he just figured this out? Considering the phone calls she'd been getting from some of her favorite designers, trouble had been brewing for some time.

The waitress brought Kenzie her brownie and Sam his gluten-free muffin. She bit into the brownie, the chocolate practically exploding on her tongue. Hendrix was a wizard with chocolate.

Sam neatly sliced the muffin and tentatively took a bite. He chewed cautiously and then smiled. "Delicious."

"Hendrix is an amazing pastry chef." She licked

her fingers, eyes half-closed in satisfaction. Kenzie was so happy Donovan and Hendrix were getting married. She was going to have brownies like this for the rest of her life.

Sam took a sip of his coffee. "The reason I'm here is...I've been authorized to offer you anything you want to get you back to New York."

Her eyebrows rose. "Anything?"

"Well, within reason."

"Double my salary."

"Done." He grinned happily.

"Fifty-thousand-dollar clothing budget?"

"Done."

"First-class air travel."

"Done."

"Two personal assistants of my own choosing."

Sam grinned. "Done."

"And they get their own clothing budget. I think ten thousand should do it for them."

He hesitated, but then smiled. "Done."

"Broadway tickets to theaters of my choice and a private box."

"How many shows are we talking about?"

"At least six."

"Four," he said.

"I can go with four."

"I will have Legal send you a contract by the end of business today."

She stood up. "Don't bother. I don't want the job."

His mouth fell open in astonishment. "But... but..."

"No." She turned, waving at the waitress, and headed back to her store.

* * *

It took Sam ten minutes to get over his shock and track her down. He stood in front of her waiting while she finished ringing up a sale. She handed the package to the customer and then turned to him.

"What do you mean, no?"

"What part of the word *no* don't you understand? I don't want to work for them, and I don't want to work with you." She turned to a mannequin and neatly adjusted the drape of the skirt.

"Your grandmother would understand. She doesn't need you."

She frowned at him. "Maybe I need her." Didn't he understand she was building something for herself? If she went back to her old job, she'd be building something for other people.

"I can be what you need." He sounded desperate.

"No, you can't." She wondered what his promise was to get her back. Even though she was really good at her job, she was just another cog in the big, corporate machine. "I may not have known this when I was with you, but I was just your accessory, a stepping-stone to helping you up the next rung in the corporate ladder."

"Don't you want to run things?" he asked curiously.

She gestured at the store. "I already do." She made all the decisions on the running of the boutiques. "Why would I go back? I would be taking a step back instead of a step forward. Not only career-wise, but with my personal life."

His eyes narrowed. "Are you dating someone?"

"As if you weren't five seconds after I moved out of your apartment."

"If you're talking about Denise, that's over already."

"Why? Wasn't she being helpful enough in furthering your career?"

"That is mean and petty, Kenzie. You're not mean and petty."

"I moved on. You should, too. It builds character."

"No one does this to me," he moaned.

She waved her hand, tired of the conversation. "Already done."

He grabbed her arm tightly and jerked her toward him. "I said no one does this to me."

A hand shot out and grabbed Sam's pinky, bending it back. "Let Kenzie go." Reed's voice was deep and menacing.

"Ow!" Sam let go of Kenzie and rubbed his hand.

Even though she knew Sam had a temper, he had never manhandled her before and she quivered with anger. "Get out, Sam."

"But, Kenzie," he whined.

"The lady said to leave," Reed said quietly.

Sam turned and took a step. He glanced back at Kenzie. "This isn't over." Then he left.

Reed watched the man leave before turning back to Kenzie, working to control his fury that someone would attempt to hurt her. "Are you all right?"

She nodded rubbing her arm. "I'm a little in shock, but I'm fine."

"Has this happened before?"

"No. Never." She smiled. "Thank you for rescuing me, but in another half second my martial arts training would have kicked in and Sam would have been on the floor."

"I have absolutely no doubt. Come on," he said. "Your grandmother called a meeting and you didn't answer your phone. So I came to collect you." Sam! So that man was her infamous ex. He was surprised that Kenzie would choose someone so...so petty.

They walked out into the lobby and Reed saw her ex waiting for an elevator. A rush of anger returned. He wasn't a violent man, but if that jerk looked even cross-eyed at Kenzie, Reed would beat him to a pulp and then turn him over to her brothers.

"What's going on?" Kenzie asked as they pushed open the door that led to the offices and the meeting rooms behind the lobby.

"Are you sure you don't want to talk about what just happened?" he asked.

"Not now." She walked down the long hallway to the conference room.

Miss E. sat at the head of the table with Jasper on her left. Scott prowled the room like a caged jaguar. Hunter poured coffee. He looked tired, as if he hadn't slept for several nights. Donovan sat looking curious, a smudge of flour on his face and a bit of lipstick at the corner of his lips.

Jasper looked old. Even though he was only in his mid-seventies, he looked as though he'd aged a decade.

Kenzie sat down and Reed took the chair next to her. Miss E. held up a hand. Scott and Hunter sat down.

"Jasper has some information," Miss E. said. Her voice sounded almost sad.

Miss E.'s eyes looked tired, too, and she kept glancing at Jasper with affection tinged with unhappiness.

Jasper clasped his hands in front of him. He glanced at Miss E. and she nodded.

"This isn't easy," Jasper started and stopped. He swallowed. "But I thought the name Preferred Investments sounded familiar, and it was, because..." He stopped and ran a hand over his face. "My daughter is the majority shareholder in Nevada Investment Reserves. There's a connection."

Everyone went quiet. Scott leaned toward his grandmother. "Tell me."

Miss E. took a deep breath. "She's the one, we think, who has been behind some of the problems we've been having."

"You know, when you see lots of little things and they don't mean anything," Jasper said, "I started thinking about Louisa and the fact that she had possessions that cost way more than I could account for. I knew she was angry when I decided to put the casino up as the prize in the poker tournament, but I didn't know how angry."

Miss E. patted his hand. "I'm sorry, Jasper. I know this is hard."

"How did you find out?" Scott said. "I'm still trying to trace all the transactions that went through Preferred Investments."

"The name Preferred Investments sounded so familiar, but I couldn't place it. I knew I'd seen the name somewhere. I started going through my files and I finally located it. Several years ago, Louisa said she was starting a company and was putting her legal affairs in order. She was doing her last will and testament and wanted to give me and her mother shared power of attorney in case something happened to her. I didn't think anything of it at the time, though I was proud of her for getting the whole will and such done. Eventually she gave me a copy of her will and in it was a list of her investments. Preferred Investments was on that list."

Scott nodded his head and Reed found himself mimicking Scott's action.

"We need to talk to Louisa. Where is she?"

"She left on a cruise of the Caribbean last week and won't be home until next Monday."

"Does anybody know why?" Kenzie asked.

"I think that's a question we need to ask her," Scott replied.

Jasper cleared his throat. "Louisa liked being the daughter of a man who owned a casino. That gave her a level of respect that she craved. She always had money." He frowned. "Even though money and respect didn't seem enough to make Louisa happy. I spoiled her." His voice trailed away. "I wanted her to have a happy, fun-filled childhood and I never figured she'd grow up to be a thief. I guess I was wrong."

"Stop," Miss E. ordered. "There is a point in any person's life where acting badly becomes a choice, not an excuse. We all know the difference between right and wrong and Louisa knew that, too. Why else would she hide her behavior?"

"What are we going to do about her?" Kenzie asked. "She's committed fraud and I don't even know what else she's done that's a felony."

"She's my daughter," Jasper pleaded. "I can't let her go to jail."

"You may not have a choice," Scott said quietly. "The state of Nevada is very sensitive about any wrongdoing that affects gambling. People come here thinking they have a chance at the big win and if they think we're cheating them, they'll stop coming."

Jasper looked down at his hands, misery stark on his face. "What if I made restitution?"

"You mean bail her out, again?" Scott said, his voice harsh.

"We're not sending her to jail," Miss E. said firmly. "Scott, find another way to deal with this. Jasper, we're not going to let her go to jail, but we're not letting her get away with this."

Reed's father would have made him go to jail if he'd messed up like this, no matter what hits his own reputation took. His by-the-book father would have been there for him, but he wouldn't hide behind the excuse of Reed not knowing right from wrong.

Scott tapped on his tablet. "Give me a while and I'll track down all her bank accounts. If she agrees to make restitution and get some help, we could work with that."

"What kind of restitution?" Jasper asked.

"Give me some time to think about that," Scott said. "I'm not in the business of forgiveness." He pushed away from the table and stood. He refilled his mug with coffee and glanced at the sideboard. "Where are the treats, Donovan?"

"Didn't have time," Donovan said.

"I don't know about you," Miss E. said, "but I need a shower and a brownie."

Reed scooted back, as well. "Let's get some lunch," he said to Kenzie.

She nodded and waved goodbye to her grandmother and brothers.

"I feel sorry for Jasper," Kenzie said after the waitress set her hamburger down in front of her. "He loves his daughter and living with the guilt of her sins is going to be difficult. He has to look at us every day and know what his daughter did to cripple us."

"Your grandmother handled the situation with great restraint."

"Where was that restraint when we were growing up?" Kenzie said with a grin. "We behaved well because we knew there were consequences. My grandmother may look like a sweet little old lady, but she would not hesitate to make us pay for our sins with an iron fist. If I'd done what Louisa did, I'd be a night janitor in the hotel for the rest of my life."

"But you wouldn't," Reed said as he dug into his hamburger. The French fries were done exactly the way he liked them. He poured ketchup over the steaming fries.

"But I thought about things," Kenzie said with a wry chuckle. "I knew some buyers in bad financial straits who sold designer samples on eBay even though that was against company policy. People did it anyway. Not me, though."

"And you let that go?" Reed asked curiously. He'd had a few employees who'd developed software on their own time. He could have claimed their development, but he didn't.

"It was the difference between eating or paying

rent," Kenzie replied. "For Jasper's daughter the choice is 'Ooh! Do I want Prada or Louis Vuitton?'"

"You sound angry."

"I'm angry for my grandmother and Jasper. Jasper's a nice man. No matter what Louisa has done, he will never stop loving her."

"And Miss E. wouldn't love you if you did something untoward?"

"She'd love me in my orange jumpsuit, but I'd still pay for my actions."

"Ouch!" Reed said. "Your family constantly surprises me." Reed had friends who did nothing but fight with their families. To see the Russell family cooperate in such a smooth manner made him want to be a part of it.

"You shouldn't be surprised. We've had our rivalries, but when push comes to shove, we're a line nobody else can cross."

Reed had that same kind of relationship with his father. "I grew up seeing a lot of stressed-out military families. My dad was able to keep everything together and I always wondered how he did it." He remembered the stress of moving from one assignment to another, moving across country to the Pentagon and from the Pentagon to another base and then another. His childhood had been five schools in ten years. The first time he'd stayed in one place for more than two years had been high school. While many military children adapted easily, Reed had always felt awkward moving to yet another school and having to make friends all over again.

Kenzie thought for a moment. "There's something to be said about stability, but I think the idea of moving and remaking yourself every couple of years is kind of exciting. Fashion is all about remaking the line to accommodate each season and the new trends that spring up. I had to figure out what women were going to buy and why."

"I had to figure things out from the point of view of technology, and technology seems to change faster than fashion. And that was pressure." Pressure he was happy to leave behind. He could enjoy the little things in life and one of the things he was enjoying was Kenzie.

He liked everything about her. He liked the way she looked at him. The way she treasured her independence, her can-do spirit. He especially liked the way she loved her grandmother, her brothers, her two nieces and her sister-in-law. Family was important to her. He'd made his own place in her family, but his place wasn't quite the same as hers. She belonged and he was an outsider who'd made a connection with them.

"You're thinking too hard," Kenzie said, putting her hand over his. "Where are we going, Reed? You and I?"

Her hand was warm and a delicate contrast against his skin. He turned her question over and over in his mind. "I like being with you. I like the way you think, the way you talk and the way you look. I want something real. Something real with you. You're real." He stood, sliding out of the booth and holding out his hand. "Let's go to the circus. Circus Esperanza is in town. Arrived yesterday."

"I do owe you a 'good time' under the big top."

His eyebrows jiggled. "Yes, you do. Maybe you

can buy a trapeze and we can try it out some night. How hard can sex be in the air?"

She just laughed. "Harder than you think. I'll stick to pirate costumes."

The memory of her in her costume started his heart beating super hard.

She slid out of the booth, grinning at him. "I need to change and then we can go."

He glanced down at his suit. "Me, too." He took her hand and led her to the elevators.

Chapter 13

Kenzie watched the clowns race around the center ring doing somersaults, rolling in the sawdust, shooting water at each other. The audience laughed uproariously. A part of her had always been apprehensive around clowns. Who knew what was under all that face paint that made each one look jovial and silly?

Next to her on the bench, Reed munched on popcorn. At each antic, he burst out into laughter. He looked as if he was ten years old and was so irresistibly charming, she felt a lurch in her heart and a shiver of excitement. *I'm in love with him.*

After one exuberant laugh, a lock of blond hair fell into his eyes and she wanted to push it back the way her grandmother had always done for her and her brothers.

Reed was a beautiful man and he had absolutely

no idea he was. He really didn't understand about the women he said were attracted to his money. She was sure money was part of the attraction, but he had a kindness to him, a way of making people feel important. His innate charm was what attracted people to him.

He'd commented on the chaos of his childhood as a military dependent, but those experiences had made him what he was. He could look at chaos calmly. He could examine every side of a problem and find a solution that satisfied everyone. He was quietly tenacious. People turned to him knowing he would find the answer. Sam rushed in to solve a problem because he needed it done. Reed was more cautious. Kenzie went with her gut. Her gut was telling her now that Reed was the right man for her. She was in love with him. The thought scared her.

He was the kind of man who wanted a lifetime commitment. She didn't know if she was ready for one.

The clowns gave way to the dancing dogs. Kenzie watched, laughing in the appropriate places, but her thoughts were miles away. How did she tell this man she loved him? Their backgrounds were so different. He went to MIT and she went to UCLA. He was changing the world and she was just making it look pretty. Other than the hotel and casino and her grandmother, they had nothing in common. But then again, she and Sam had everything in common and they couldn't make their relationship work.

Her attention was drawn back to the center ring. Acrobats tossed themselves around while aerialists sailed overhead. Elephants paraded around the outer

edge of the three rings, and women in feathered head-
dresses and sparkly outfits swayed back and forth
from their perches behind the elephants' ears. The
music rose to a crescendo and as the acts took their
final bows, people started to stand and make their
ways to the folded back openings at either end of the
huge tent.

The show was over.

"Are you okay?" Reed asked when they were back
in his car and heading back to the Mariposa.

"I'm fine. I need to talk to my grandmother about
something. Can you drop me off at her RV?"

"Of course."

At Kenzie's knock, Miss E. opened her door. Light
from inside streamed out as Kenzie smiled at her
grandmother. She wore a faded blue chenille robe
she'd had since Kenzie could remember.

"Do you have a moment?"

Miss E. stepped away from the door and let Kenzie in.

"Would you like some tea?" her grandmother
asked.

"I'd love some." Kenzie settled herself on the sofa
while Miss E. busied herself in the tiny galley.

Kenzie composed her thoughts.

"I thought you were going out with Reed tonight?"
Miss E. set a cup of tea on the side table. She added
a plate of Hendrix's brownies.

"We went to the circus."

"The circus. You've never wanted to go before because you were afraid of clowns. Though from what
I've read, a lot of people find clowns uncomfortable.

Which reminds me of when you were young and we would have tea while you worked out your problems."

Kenzie took a sip. "I have feelings for Reed," she blurted out.

"And that's a problem?"

"I thought I loved Sam and look how that turned out."

"You didn't love Sam."

"Really!" Kenzie's eyebrows rose in surprise. "It certainly felt like love."

Miss E. took a bite out of a brownie. She leaned back in her recliner, studying Kenzie. "Sam was a learning experience. Mistakes are only mistakes when you don't learn from them. What did you learn from your relationship with him?"

"Never date a man who takes more time in the bathroom to get ready than you do." Reed got ready in ten minutes. No primping in front of the mirror for him to make sure every wave in his hair was perfectly positioned.

"What else did you learn?" Miss E.'s lips quirked at the edges as though trying to suppress a smile.

"Never date a man who doesn't understand your love for your family." And who accused her of being selfish because of her feelings.

Miss E. nodded. "Exactly."

"Sam wasn't a team player unless you were on his team and supporting him. If I didn't support him in anything, he sulked and made me feel miserable because I had a different perspective." In retrospect Sam was a little boy in so many ways. Reed was a man. He didn't sulk, he didn't get angry if she differed in her opinion of something and he didn't blame her if things went wrong.

"In Sam's favor," Miss E. said, "he is very charming."

"But you told me once never to trust charming."

"And you were at that stage when you wouldn't listen to me."

"I was fifteen and you were the enemy."

Miss E. burst out laughing. "I wasn't the enemy. I was your grandmother with a wealth of experience and knowledge. You just needed time for everything to percolate."

"That's the nicest way you've ever said 'I told you so,'" Kenzie said with a laugh.

"Thank you." Miss E. regally nodded.

"But Reed…"

"I like Reed. Your brothers like Reed. You like Reed. It isn't going to get any better than that." Miss E. took another bite of her brownie.

Kenzie sighed. "I think I love him. But…"

"Then you need to do something about it. But like always, Kenzie, for you things take time. Be careful. Don't overthink this."

"In other words, I need to just go on with my day."

Miss E. reached over and patted her cheek. "Exactly."

"Thank you for the advice…"

"I didn't give you any advice, I just helped you come to the same conclusion you would have come to after you'd worried for two or three days. Tell Reed how you feel. I think you'll be very surprised at what he says in response."

Kenzie tapped her fingers nervously on the conference table. Miss E. sat at the head of the table, a cup of tea in front of her with a half-eaten cookie on a plate. Kenzie's stomach was in knots. She hadn't seen

Reed for several days and she felt awkward having finally verbalized her feelings for him. Her brothers sat around the table. Lydia talked quietly with Hunter. The tenderness on Hunter's face made Kenzie gawk at him. Her big brother, the one who'd teased her unmercifully in their childhood, was in love. Lydia looked serene and Hunter looked happy. She wanted that. She wanted that with Reed.

Scott and Donovan leaned against the buffet munching on brownies. Scott grinned at something Donovan said and they turned and headed to their chairs.

Reed opened the door and walked in. He scanned the room and when his gaze lit on Kenzie a broad smile appeared. He grabbed a cookie from the sideboard and a bottle of water and sat next to her.

"I can't help feeling angry," Kenzie said to him.

Reed opened his laptop. The screen came to life and he tapped his password and a spreadsheet appeared. "That's natural. I've spent the past few days tracking down every bank account Louisa has and she's a very wealthy woman. She didn't need more money. Her trust fund alone has nearly twenty million. Her mother is easily worth twice that from the divorce settlement and has gone on to marry and divorce richer guys than Jasper." He frowned at the screen.

"I know Miss E. has feelings for Jasper and is trying to make the best of this situation, but I can't help but think that if it were any one of us orange would be our new favorite color."

"Get everything out now," Reed said. "By the time she and Jasper arrive, you need to be calm."

"I want her punished," Scott put in.

"Scott," Miss E. said tranquilly, "she is going to be punished. We're going to take away the most important thing to her—her money. And this will get around. There will be no hiding for Louisa, and her reputation will suffer."

"I want her banned from the Mariposa," Scott said. Miss E. nodded.

"I want the money back," Kenzie added. "All that money will go a long way toward converting the amphitheater into a wedding chapel." She'd already worked out a basic floor plan for the chapel and the accompanying shops and talked to a number of designers about featuring their gowns. "I have ideas for destination weddings. Louisa is standing in the way of my genius. There was no need for her to steal one penny."

Reed patted her hand. "Angry much?"

"I am angry. How many people could I have employed and helped to stimulate the economy? She's hoarding the money for herself."

Miss E. held up a hand. "Take a breath, Kenzie. We need to be calm and rational."

The door opened and Jasper entered, his daughter in tow. Every head turned to look at her. Louisa hesitated.

"What's this?" She entered slowly, her sleek body almost catlike.

"Sit down, Louisa," Jasper said as he took his place next to Miss E.

Her gaze darted across the room. She sat, her posture stiff.

"Louisa," Miss E. said, "you need to pay back the money you stole from the casino."

Louisa's eyebrows rose. "I have no idea what you are talking about."

"Yes, you do." Disappointment showed on Jasper's face. "Don't compound the problem by denying it."

"Daddy." She shook her head. "I really don't know what you're talking about."

Scott opened a file. "You can deny it all you want, but we were finally able to trace the money you skimmed off the casino to a holding account in your name in Belgium."

"It took a lot of digging," Reed said, "but I found it. You shouldn't have used Jasper's name. We almost lost you in Hong Kong, but then I found a bank account in Belgium in your father's name with you as a signatory."

Kenzie glanced in shock at her grandmother. Miss E. was hesitating over how to deal with Louisa because Louisa had implicated her father in the theft.

"Why?" Jasper asked, sadness in his gaze.

Louisa's face twisted with anger. "The Mariposa should have been mine." Her voice rose with the depth of her anger. "I brought my friends here. I talked about the casino to everyone and urged them to come here. I worked for you to keep it afloat."

"You would have run it into the ground," Jasper said. "You've never been interested in managing all this. All you wanted was your own personal ATM. Miss E., Reed and Lydia are bringing the Mariposa back to life again. It's thriving."

"I don't have to listen to these unfounded accusations." Louisa turned, but Scott rose and went to stand in front of the door.

"Sure you do," Reed said.

"Who are you?" A brilliant smile appeared on her face. She tilted her head flirtatiously at Reed.

"I'm Reed Watson, one-third owner of the Mariposa and the man who can prove your guilt." He smiled.

"Aren't you cute," Louisa said, running a hand down her hip.

Reed simply looked disgusted and Kenzie rested her hand on his knee. Louisa had no idea how immune he was to her charm.

"I have your financial records," Reed continued. "You have a trust fund your father set up for you with twenty millions dollars in it. You have a trust fund from your grandparents with another twenty million in it. And your mother set up yet a third trust fund for you. Easily, even in today's economy, that's four million dollars a year for you to live on." Reed glanced down at the laptop screen. "Though I can understand why you find it difficult to stick to your budget when you purchase thousand-dollar bottles of champagne in one-hundred-bottle lots."

"How dare you pry into my personal business."

"How dare you take money from my pocket," Reed countered. "How dare you threaten the livelihood of every employee at the Mariposa."

Louisa lifted her chin. "I don't have time to worry about the little people."

Kenzie gasped. Her grandmother's mouth fell open in surprise.

Jasper looked shocked. "You are not my daughter."

"Promises, promises," Louisa said with an airy wave of her hand.

Miss E. stood. "You owe the Mariposa seventeen million dollars and your father an apology."

"To be exact," Reed said, "the figure is $17,400,231.13."

Louisa shrugged, tilting her head, appearing un-concerned.

Kenzie wanted to gouge her eyes out for hurting Jasper. Jasper was a nice man and didn't deserve this. He'd worked hard to give this unappreciative woman a good life and she'd repaid him by stealing from him.

"You will make restitution," Miss E. continued.

"Don't worry, Eleanor, I'll pay back the money," Jasper said.

Miss E. turned at him and glared, her hands on her hips. "No. No. You will not get your daughter out of this jam." She turned back to Louisa. "If you choose not to repay, I'll sue you in open court and the whole world will know what you did."

Louisa looked surprised. "You don't get to speak to me like this."

Miss E. marched up to the other woman and glared. "What I want to do is turn you over my knee and give you a good spanking, and I've never spanked or hurt anyone in my whole life."

Tears welled up in Louisa's eyes. Kenzie watched dispassionately. Louisa glanced at every man in the room, trying to look miserable. Kenzie glanced at Reed and realized he was grinning. A second later, Reed burst out laughing. Even Scott's lips trembled with amusement.

Miss E. started laughing, too. "Do you really think we'll be taken in by your crocodile tears?"

Louisa stiffened. The tears disappeared and anger contorted her face.

Miss E. returned to her chair and sat down. "Now, sit down, Louisa. We have a lot to discuss." She glanced at her watch. "My lawyer will be here in a moment."

On cue, Scott opened the door and Miss E.'s lawyer, Vanessa Peabody, entered.

Kenzie gave Vanessa a little wave and grinned. Vanessa sat across from Kenzie and smiled back as she opened her tote and pulled out her tablet and a file folder.

"Now," Miss E. said. "The terms of your repayment will be worked out with Miss Peabody. You are banned from the Mariposa for the rest of your life. You've caused a lot of resentment."

"I will fight this," Louisa said.

"You may if you wish," Miss E. said. "But keep in mind, some of your other secrets will come out."

"Such as?"

"Your association with a known criminal who tried to steal the ten-million-dollar jackpot from the casino last year. Your meddling in the renovations of the restaurant when you pretended to be Lydia and changed the cabinet order and the flooring. Need I go on?"

Louisa refused to look defeated. She glared at everyone. "I will sign this for you, Daddy. See, I'm a good daughter."

Jasper didn't say anything. Kenzie's heart went out to him at the sadness and hurt in his eyes. Miss E. gripped his hand tightly. He shook his head.

"I tried to be a good father to you, Louisa. I really did."

Louisa made no reply.

Chapter 14

Reed set his laptop down on the conference room table. Only that morning this room had been the site of Louisa Biggins's downfall and he couldn't help thinking about the woman and the look on her face once she'd realized her deception had been discovered. There'd been no remorse, only arrogance. Reed had reserved his pity for Jasper. His father had once told him that even good parents could have bad kids for reasons that had nothing to do with the parents.

He couldn't stop smiling as Kenzie eyed him curiously. Reed opened the laptop, turned it on and motioned her to come closer and see the presentation he'd prepared for her. He was deeply delighted he'd been able to make everything work just the way she wanted. He wanted to please her, to show her what he could do with her idea. He'd succeeded in ways he hadn't even expected. He could see a hundred different applications for the core component of the software and how it could be used in many different ways.

"So you fixed the software," she said.

His smile grew wider. He'd not only fixed, but improved the software. "Take a look."

She leaned over his arm, her orchid-and-vanilla perfume spinning about him. One of the things he liked best about her was her scent.

"Let me show you." He ran a finger over the touch pad. "I spent the morning in your store talking to some of the customers. I took their photos and Bianca chose five dresses she thought would look good on each of them." He clicked on one. "And by the way, don't ever fire her."

"I hadn't planned on it," Kenzie said, amusement in her voice.

"She can pick out women with money to burn and of the five dresses she chose for them, two of the women bought all the dresses and one bought three dresses and the last one bought one."

He clicked again and the first woman popped up. She was tall and curvy with shoulder-length brown hair swept back behind her ears. Diamonds sparkled around her neck and on her hands. "Dress number one." He dragged the dress to the woman's photo, her head superimposed over a template that was closest to her body type. He chose a dress from the open window on the side of the screen and dragged it over to her. The dress conformed perfectly to the woman's figure.

Kenzie clapped. "Wonderful." She leaned closer and he caught the sweetness of her breath.

He showed each dress Bianca had chosen for the woman and grinned when Kenzie leaned against him. He went through the other women and showed Kenzie how each template conformed to their specific body type.

"This is so perfect," Kenzie said. "I'm stunned and amazed."

"It got me thinking how perfect this would work as a phone app." He started clicking on the second woman and showing her how the dresses conformed to her shorter, more slender figure. The third woman was a plus size, as Bianca had explained to him, and each outfit looked perfect on her. "I could do this for shoes and lingerie."

Kenzie covered her mouth with her hands, her eyes wide with joy. "I knew you could fix it."

Reed turned to her and grabbed her into his arms and kissed her. She returned the kiss enthusiastically and heat spiraled outward. She wrapped her arms around his neck and pressed tight against him.

This woman had become something so much more than he'd expected. She had become not only a woman he wanted, but a partner. *I need to marry her.* For a second, he was so stunned at the thought of marriage he couldn't move forward.

"You are a genius," Kenzie said turning back to the laptop.

"I am, aren't I?"

She laughed. "And ever so humble."

"I'm going to call the app Kenzie Shops."

"I'm an app!" She clapped her hands and planted a kiss on his cheek. "It'll be on every woman's phone.

Take a selfie and then put clothes on it. Virtual paper dolls."

He would have to tinker a bit more with the app idea and pare down the coding to a more manageable size, but it could be done. Suddenly, he was anxious to get started.

"So," Kenzie said, "tell me about Scott's bachelor party."

He gazed at her. "I'm a little uncomfortable talking to you about a man's bachelor party, especially when you're his sister." He'd thrown a bachelor party for Arthur. They'd played Dungeons and Dragons for two days straight. Arthur had shown up for his wedding practically asleep until Reed had plied him with a gallon of coffee and then his best friend had been so hyper he couldn't calm down enough to say his vows.

"That's the point. I am his sister and best friend of the bride."

"You're trying to pump me for information, aren't you?"

Kenzie grinned. "I would never do something so surreptitious."

"What are you doing for the bachelorette party?"

"It will encompass wine, chocolate-covered strawberries and cheesecake, of which Nina will eat nothing because she has to fit into the dress."

"That's it? You're basically going to eat."

She nodded with a happy smile on her beautiful face. Her dark eyes sparkled as she rubbed her hands together. "That's every woman's fantasy."

"I've never seen you push away from the table."

She eyed him with a slight frown. "Was that a judgmental tone?"

Reed held up his hands. "No. I've taken dozens of women out to dinner and watch them push a three-hundred-dollar meal around on the plate. The fact that you eat makes me appreciate you even more." He silently applauded himself for getting out of that trap without messing up more. He should have learned long ago not to call attention to a woman's eating habits, but Kenzie took such delight in her food. He'd really meant it as a compliment.

"Stop looking so worried. I was just pulling your string." She laughed. "And I enjoyed it."

"I can't tell you about the bachelor party because I don't know. Hunter planned it."

"Hunter! You're probably going to hunt something big and ferocious with nothing but a toothpick and your wit." She patted his cheek. "Have fun."

"You're kidding, right?"

"Be grateful they aren't hunting you."

The look in her eyes told him she was teasing, but he couldn't help a small burst of apprehension. He'd known her brothers for such a short time he wasn't certain where he stood with them since he was dating their sister. Staying away wasn't an option. He would just have to make the best of it.

He kissed Kenzie again. "The software is already installed on the store computers. And I guess I won't see you again until tomorrow at the wedding." He sounded forlorn even to himself.

"Have a good time at the party."

"Have a good time."

He didn't intend to stop at the jewelry store situated between Kenzie's boutiques. He found himself standing in front of the store looking at the rings in the window.

"Reed Watson," a man's voice said.

Reed glanced up to find Kenzie's ex, Sam, standing next to him. "Sam Bell, right?"

Sam smiled at him. "Kenzie is never going to be happy here."

"Excuse me?" What was this man talking about?

"Here in Reno with you."

"Where should she be?" Reed asked curiously.

"Back in New York. Saks is ready to take her back at double her salary. You are preventing her from going."

Reed thought about it for a second and decided to play dumb. "I don't think I follow you."

"Kenzie needs Broadway, Times Square and decent restaurants. She's never going to be happy in this backwater town."

Kenzie seemed pretty happy to Reed. "Have you asked her what she wants?"

Sam shrugged dismissively. "She won't listen to me, but you have some influence over her, and you should do what any man would do."

"What would that be?"

"See that she's happy."

Reed's eyes narrowed. He stepped back to study Sam. The man had a look of desperation in his eyes. "I get it now. If you don't entice her back to New York, you're going to lose your job, aren't you?"

Sam looked startled. "My job isn't in jeopardy, but Kenzie's future is."

"I read some articles lately about casinos being the new big business. I'm a multimillionaire and some serious things are going to have to happen to cause me to lose my money. So basically, Kenzie has a job for as long as she wants with me."

"So you won't talk to her for me?"

"Nope. In fact, I'm going to marry her." Reed walked into the jewelry store.

He bent over a display case with engagement and wedding rings neatly arranged on white satin fabric.

"What are you doing?" Scott asked curiously.

Reed started. He hadn't heard the man enter the shop. "Just looking."

"That ring would look perfect on you." Scott pointed at a solitaire diamond surrounded by brown diamonds. Reed loved the new colors in diamonds.

"It's…it's…not for me." The last thing he wanted to admit was his feelings for Kenzie to her brother.

"It would look great on Kenzie's hand, too." Scott pointed at another ring. "Kenzie would like that one more. Wait. Wait. I need to call Hunter and Donovan, we're going to help you."

Reed wasn't certain he liked that at all. Soon, Donovan sauntered into the jewelry store, followed a few minutes after that by Hunter.

"What's all this about?" Hunter asked as he glanced around the store.

"We are standing in for Nina?" At the confused look on Reed's face, Scott added, "If Nina wasn't marrying me tomorrow, she'd be helping Reed pick out an engagement ring for Kenzie."

Reed felt claustrophobic with Kenzie's brothers clustered around him. The jewelry store wasn't that large and most of the available space was taken up with glass display cases.

"Are we making this the bachelor party?" Hunter asked, leaning over a case and smiling at a delicate chain necklace.

"This is the start," Scott said. "After this, we're heading out for dinner and drinks."

"Actually," Donovan interrupted, "we're heading to my house. I'm making dinner. Hendrix already made the dessert."

"Is there going to be room for all of us and Nina's brothers?" Scott asked. "She has five of them. And don't forget Jasper, and Nina's dad, who I assume is already there cooking up a storm."

"Yeah," Donovan added. "Dinner tonight is a complete meal of Brazilian dishes with unpronounceable names."

Reed had met Manny Torres and sampled some of his Brazilian dishes. Manny was a chef whose food was inspired by his Brazilian roots.

"The kitchen is huge," Donovan said. "There's room for a small army in it."

"And brownies, I hope," Hunter said.

"Brownies, pies, cookies and chocolate mousse. We have choices. I didn't know what Nina's brothers would like so Hendrix made a huge assortment of desserts and stocked a full bar."

Reed felt as if he was suffocating. He'd only stopped in on the spur of the moment and suddenly Kenzie's brothers were taking charge. This was not what he envisioned.

The brothers dispersed to the different cases, leaning over each one and pointing out what they thought Kenzie would like.

"So when are you popping the question?" Donovan asked as he nodded to the saleswoman.

Reed drew back startled. "I wasn't even planning on shopping for a ring yet. I was just looking." If Kenzie said yes, he would be marrying her and, in some ways, her family. Once thing he'd admired about the Russell family was their closeness. They had barbecues weekly and it seemed they were all in each other's business. While he'd envied their closeness, he hadn't thought about how it would affect him.

"We're just here to help you look." Scott pointed at a ring and nodded at the saleswoman.

Reed was almost too uncomfortable to focus on what he wanted.

Donovan patted him on the shoulder. "I know we can be overwhelming at times, but we're cool with you and Kenzie."

The choices were so immense. Reed pointed at a ring. "Kenzie likes rubies, doesn't she?"

"She likes diamonds, too," Hunter offered.

"What's your budget?" Scott asked.

Reed hadn't even thought about a budget. Until fifteen minutes ago, he'd been browsing to see what the choices were. He hesitated, aware that the three men eyed him curiously. "I only decided a couple hours ago that I wanted to marry her."

"We're not railroading you," Hunter added. "If you need to take longer to think about your decision, we're okay with that. But since we're all here…"

"I don't have a budget." Reed knew that a million-dollar-ring would never impress Kenzie. Even though Kenzie was deeply aware of fashion, her own clothing choices tended to be simple, yet still elegant. He wanted an engagement ring that reflected her own fashion tastes.

"Okay," Scott said, leaning over Reed's choice. "Kenzie loves red with sparklies. Look at those rubies. I like this one." Scott motioned to the salesgirl, who inserted her key and opened the back of the display case.

She set Scott's choices on a black velvet cloth. "I think Miss Kenzie would like these choices, but I think she would love this one. I'm just confirming, there are no budget considerations?"

"Really?" he asked. She knew who he was.

"Mr. Watson," the woman said with a pleasant smile, "Miss Kenzie stole me from Neiman's jewelry department. I am a well-trained employee and we have been instructed to ask no matter who the customer is."

"There are no budget considerations."

"Thank you." The woman put away all the rings Reed had looked at and then turned to the display behind her and opened the glass door. She pulled out a ring and set it down on the velvet square. "I think you should consider this one. We've all tried this on and Miss Kenzie practically drooled over it. And it's her size. You won't need to resize it."

Scott leaned over and whispered, "You were just schooled by the jewelry lady."

"Can we just let me be embarrassed silently?"

Scott grinned. "That would be a no."

Hunter nodded and Donovan clapped him on the back. They all clustered around the ring sitting on the black velvet.

Reed was in. He'd won the brothers over.

A huge heart-shaped ruby sat in a setting of black gold and was framed by alternating diamonds and rubies in a channel that went completely around the setting. Delicate scrolling had been etched into the sides. Reed knew. He just knew. He nodded at the woman and handed her his American Express credit card.

"The center ruby is four carats," the sales woman said. "The total weight of the other rubies and diamonds is another two carats. And…you also get the employee discount of thirty percent."

Reed picked up the ring. This was the one. Kenzie would love it. The ring was elegant and classy in a way that suited her. He was mostly sold on the unique quality of it, a quality that matched Kenzie. This ring was perfect.

"I definitely want this one," he said. Eighty thousand dollars wasn't a bad price.

"Perfect," Scott said.

Donovan picked the ring up, studied it and then nodded before passing the ring to Hunter.

Hunter smiled and handed it to the saleswoman. "This is the one. Pack it up for Reed."

The woman accepted the ring back, smiling as she headed toward the register.

"If I get a discount, does that impact your commission?" Reed asked as he followed her to the back of the shop.

She gave him an odd look. "Is that a proper question to ask?"

He looked at her name tag. "Claudia, I walked in, you sized me up, knew exactly who I was, and told me what Kenzie would want because you know her that well. Which means you're excellent at your job, because Kenzie is picky. If the discount cuts into your commission, then no. I don't want it. You earned every penny of your commission today."

"Then no discount," Claudia said with a sweet smile. "Kenzie is a very lucky woman." She turned back to the display and pulled out two other rings. "These are the matching wedding rings."

The bands of both rings were plain black gold. Instead of gems, they had delicate scrolling etched into them. The man's ring was too big for Reed and would have to be resized. "Shall I set these two rings in the safe for you to pick up later?"

"Yes, please." He'd never been humbled by a salesperson before. What that told him was that Kenzie knew how to hire her people.

He walked out of the jewelry store with the ring burning a hole in his pocket. Her brothers bracketed him as they walked through the lobby.

"How do you feel?" Scott asked.

"Excited, anxious, hopeful, frightened."

Hunter laughed. "It's love. Welcome to the family."

Kenzie sipped a glass of champagne. Nina sat across from her on Lydia's cream-colored leather sofa.

"Here," Nina said handing small gift boxes to Kenzie, Maya and Nina's sister, Lola. Lola looked enough like Nina to be her twin even though she was five years younger.

"Sparklies," Kenzie said, sliding a thumbnail under the edge of the wrapping paper. She opened the hinged box to show a solitaire sapphire on a white gold chain. "It's perfect. And matches our dresses."

"That's the point," Nina said with a wry chuckle.

Her mother, Grace Torres, came out of the kitchen bearing a tray of food, followed by Miss E. who carried two bottles of champagne. Lydia's mother, Caroline, carried another tray of food followed by Hendrix pushing a cart filled with desserts that sent up a smell so heavenly Kenzie's mouth started to water. She wondered how much she could eat tonight and still fit in her bridesmaid dress tomorrow.

"You're so calm," Kenzie said. "When you married Carl, you were insane."

"Marrying Carl was the wrong decision. Now I'm on the right track." Nina munched on carrot sticks lathered with almond butter.

"I noticed. There's no need for bridezilla hysterics."

Hendrix was next on the list. She wanted a Christmas wedding. And from the way Miss E. had been keeping company with Jasper, she was about to fall, too. Kenzie felt a little left out. She saw her family moving on with their lives and she felt as if she was in a holding pattern with Reed. That thought made her feel odd.

"You seem a little off tonight," Nina said to Kenzie.

"I thought I was in love with Sam. With Reed, I don't know." Her feelings for Reed were deep and when she was with him she didn't want to leave him.

"Stop second-guessing yourself," Miss E. said.

"I'm not." Kenzie reached for a bottle and refilled her champagne flute. The bubbles tickled her nose as she drank.

"You want everything to be perfect," Nina said, "and it isn't going to be."

"I don't want things to be perfect, I just don't know his feelings for me. I think I'm in love with him. No, I know I'm in love with him." Now that she'd said the words out loud she felt relief.

"So, my darling," Miss E. said, her tone soft and kind, "what's the problem?"

What was the problem? She turned the words over and over in her head. Looking back she saw all the signs that said Sam had been Mr. Right Now. Reed was Mr. Right. He was a different kind of commitment that promised to last a lifetime and she was afraid.

"What are you afraid of?" Miss E. asked. She sat next Kenzie and put her arm around her.

"Failure," Kenzie whispered. "I'm afraid of failure."

"There is no guarantee that anything will last, but if you don't take the leap, you'll never know."

Kenzie hugged her grandmother tightly. "I've always thought failure is not trying."

"Not trying at all is guaranteed failure." Miss E. kissed her. "Go with your heart, Kenzie."

Kenzie kissed her grandmother back and turned to Nina. "All right, let's get this party on the road."

Chapter 15

The banquet room had been transformed into a slice of heaven with huge floral arrangements and white ribbon. One end held a small stage with an arbor decorated in white roses and a blue flower Kenzie didn't recognize. Kenzie stood to one side, grinning at Nina, who looked radiant in her gown, a crown of flowers woven through her hair and a small veil that swept down to her waist. Scott beamed at her as he repeated his vows. He wore a black tuxedo that gave him a distinguished air. Kenzie thought he was the handsomest man in the room except for Reed.

Her gaze swept the rows of chairs and she saw Reed sitting behind Miss E. Miss E. looked amazing in a flowing gold gown that hugged her figure. Her white hair had been swept up into an elegant French roll. She looked so happy with Jasper seated next to her. Lydia sat next to Jasper, the baby asleep in her lap.

The other side of the room held the whole Torres family. Grace wore a bright blue silk caftan with silver lace around the hem and up the front. She'd bought the caftan in Morocco and confided in Kenzie that she'd saved it for this moment. Manny Torres wore a black tuxedo with a silver bow tie to match his wife. Nina's brothers sat behind their parents looking very handsome as they watched the ceremony.

The vows finished, the music started and Nina and Scott faced their room. Kenzie was so happy for her best friend. Kenzie handed back her bouquet of orchids and roses. Maya stepped in front of them with her basket of rose petals and started throwing them down on the white runner. Kenzie took Hunter's arm, Lola took Donovan's arm and they followed Nina and Scott down the aisle formed between the chairs to the back of the hall where tables had been set for their meal. People threw confetti over the newly married couple and Kenzie grinned back at Reed when he grinned at her.

They formed a reception line to greet all the guests. Several of Nina's clients kissed her as they moved down the line. Carl, Nina's ex-husband, kissed her enthusiastically and his new wife, Anastasia, looked as if she was crying. When all the guests had been greeted and thanked for coming, the photographer took the wedding party outside for photos.

"Are you enjoying yourself?" Kenzie asked Reed once they were seated for dinner. Hotel staff moved back and forth around the tables delivering the first course.

"I am," he replied. "This is a sophisticated party that is splash fun. Those two things rarely come together. And the bride and groom look happy."

Nina and Scott sat at their own table in the center of the room flanked by Nina's parents on one side and Miss E. on the other "They do, don't they? My brother has no idea what he's gotten himself into."

"Is that a good or a bad thing?"

"For Scott, it's a good thing. That man likes to control his universe and now he's going to find out how much fun it is to throw that out the window." Kenzie smiled at her brother. Scott had changed in the months since he'd met Nina. He wasn't so rigid, so inflexible. He looked relaxed. He'd seldom looked peaceful before.

"I wanted to tell you that your friend Sam stopped me in the lobby yesterday."

"What did Sam have to say?" Sam had a lot of balls, talking to Reed.

"He says I should release you from your job here, and let you go back to New York because you're miserable."

"I'm miserable?" She swept her hand across her forehead. "I'm glad somebody told me. I hate the idea that I'm supposed to be unhappy when I'm not."

"I didn't think you were, but Sam was pretty insistent." Reed grinned at her.

"What did you tell him?" She picked at her salad. If she saw Sam in the next ten minutes she'd choke him.

"That number one, your job is secure because casinos are the new ATMs. And number two, you can make your own decisions and I think you already did."

"I'm not going back to New York."

"I didn't think you would. But Sam…" His voice trailed away as he shrugged.

"…thinks he knows what's best for me." Kenzie finished for him. "He doesn't."

"I didn't think so."

The second course came and then the main course. Manny Torres spoke briefly about his daughter, congratulating her on a husband well-chosen.

"What do you want?" Reed said after Nina's father's speech.

"I want to have balance in my life." She didn't have that in New York. But here with her family, she did. And being together again with her brothers and Miss E. showed her that family was too important to ignore. "I don't want to lose the connection to my family again. And I want…" She couldn't tell him that she loved him. At least not yet.

The photographer walked around the room taking photos while his video tech interviewed the guests about their memories of Nina and Scott. He approached Kenzie and smiled at her. "I understand you and Nina are best friends."

Kenzie nodded. "We've known each other since college."

"I'd like to interview you, if you don't mind."

"I'd like that."

He set the camera up and pinned a small mic to her dress. She found herself talking about Nina and their years in school and how they kept up their friendship afterward. She talked about the times she spent being feasted in Nina's family restaurant, serenaded by Grace and teased by her brothers. She wanted only happy memories for Nina.

After the meal, the band started up again. Nina and Scott stood in the area cleared for dancing. Their first dance. They danced with each other and then Manny and Grace, Miss E. and Hunter started dancing. After a few more minutes, Reed swung Kenzie onto the dance floor.

Everything was perfect.

"Let's take a walk," Reed said during a lull in the dancing. He gestured at the doors open to the pool area and the lighted path leading to the spa.

"Okay," she said. She was a bit warm and the cool evening breeze slid over her skin.

Reed took her hand and led her down a lighted path toward the hot springs. Steam curled up from the hot water. Stars twinkled overhead. The night sky was clear and bright. The moon sparkled on the water.

"It's beautiful here," Kenzie said.

"It's perfect." His slid an arm around her. She raised her face and he kissed her. His breath was slightly spicy from dinner.

"Perfect for what?" she asked when she drew back slightly. She shivered and he took off his jacket and draped it around her.

"The perfect end to a perfect evening."

She eyed him curiously. He suddenly seemed nervous. He ran a hand through his hair and tugged at his tie as though it were too tight.

"Kenzie… I… I…" He rubbed his forehead. "I've never done this before."

She tilted her head on him, joy bubbling up inside

her. She'd never seen him so tense before. "You've never told a woman you loved her before."

His eyes widened in surprise. "Yeah...that."

"I thought I loved Sam, but I never knew what true love was until I met and fell in love with you."

He took a deep breath. From his pocket he pulled out a small box and opened it. "Will you marry me?" He took the ring out of the box and held it up for her to see.

She gasped. How had he known how much she loved that particular ring? "Yes. I love you so much."

He slid the ring on her finger and she threw her arms around his neck and kissed him. "I am so honored. I'm going to love you forever."

"I hope so, because I'm not giving the ring back."

He kissed her hungrily and she leaned into his warmth.

"We're going to have to keep this a secret for bit. This is Nina's day."

He hugged her to him. "I know, but she probably already knows. And Lydia and Hendrix." She raised her eyebrows. "Your brothers helped me pick out the ring."

"Of course they did." She started laughing. "That's what brothers are for."

They headed back and she held his hand tightly. She didn't believe how happy she was.

Maya ran up to them, her dress flaring out behind her. "Come on, they're cutting the cake."

Reed kissed her one last time. As they entered the banquet room, she saw Scott and Hunter looking at them. Reed nodded at them and Hunter broke into a huge smile. Scott grinned and turned back to Nina, ready to cut the cake.

"I love you," Reed whispered as they watched Nina, with Scott's hand over hers, slide the knife into the wedding cake.

"I love you," she whispered back.

* * * * *

REQUEST YOUR FREE BOOKS!

2 FREE NOVELS
PLUS 2 FREE GIFTS!

KIMANI™
ROMANCE

Love's ultimate destination!

THE WORLD IS BETTER WITH

Romance

Harlequin has everything from contemporary, passionate and heartwarming to suspenseful and inspirational stories.

Whatever your mood,
we have a romance just for you!

April Knight crouched next to a young girl who sat with
a cello positioned between her spaced knees. The large,
slightly scarred instrument dwarfed her, but the teen
didn't seem intimidated. She looked on intently as, with
her signature calmness, April corrected whatever misstep
the girl had just made on the piece they were practicing.
She instructed her on how to glide the bow along the
taut strings. The result was fluid. A mesmerizing note
resonated throughout the space.

Once she was done assisting the room's lone cello
player, April returned to the front of the room. When
she turned and spotted him, her face lit up with a smile.
Several of the students—those who were not engrossed
in reading their sheet music—turned to see who had

captured their teacher's attention. April held up a hand and mouthed *five minutes*.

Damien nodded. Leaning a shoulder along the door-jamb, he folded his arms across his chest, crossed his ankles and studied the woman standing at the helm of the class. It had been months since he'd seen her, from the time when he had run into her at a Christmas party that one of his clients had invited him to at a loft in the Warehouse District. That had been what? Six months ago?

He'd arrived late, and April had been on her way out. Their encounter had been nothing more than a quick hug and profuse thanks from April for the donation Damien had given to A Fresh Start. They'd both promised each other that they would meet for coffee so they could catch up, but whenever he'd thought about calling her over the past six months something else had always come up.

Five minutes came and went, but Damien didn't dare interrupt April as she coached her pupils through a delicate piece. Besides, watching her in action was too entertaining to bring it to an end.

And to Damien's surprise he was watching her with more interest than he ever remembered watching his friend before. She wore soft yellow capri pants that hit just past her calves, a smart choice on this warm day. She probably had the heat and humidity in mind when she chose to pair it with the sleeveless white button-down blouse, but Damien thought it was the right choice for an entirely different reason.

Don't miss
PASSION'S SONG by Farrah Rochon,
available February 2016 wherever
Harlequin® Kimani Romance™ books and ebooks are sold.